DONNA SIGGERS

Betrayal

Book Two of the Warwick Cooper Thrillers

Copyright © 2019 by Donna Siggers

All rights reserved. No part of this publication may be reproduced, stored or transmitted in any form or by any means, electronic, mechanical, photocopying, recording, scanning, or otherwise without written permission from the publisher. It is illegal to copy this book, post it to a website, or distribute it by any other means without permission.

This novel is entirely a work of fiction. The names, characters and incidents portrayed in it are the work of the author's imagination. Any resemblance to actual persons, living or dead, events or localities is entirely coincidental.

Donna Siggers asserts the moral right to be identified as the author of this work.

First edition

ISBN: 9781790840359

This book was professionally typeset on Reedsy. Find out more at reedsy.com

For my wonderful children. Thank you for making me so incredibly proud, for being so diverse and excelling in all that you do. For always being there for me, especially during those tough years after my injury – you are all so amazing and I love each and every one of you

Acknowledgement

Foremost a huge thank you to my youngest daughter, Elizabeth who often loses me within the pages of whatever writing project I'm immersed. We've established a system that works, but sometimes she feels the need to threaten to confiscate my devices and ban social media!

Victoria, my eldest daughter for once again being brave enough to take on the task of editing for me and helping my seriously muddled brain to decipher a pathway of progress in my writing. Your patience with me while I'm relearning the rules of our language is truly outstanding and I cannot thank you enough for the help you've given me since my head injury to help me achieve this.

Emma and Jo, what can I say? Ladies, you lead me straight into trouble (in a good way) and I'm truly grateful for the fun we have, whatever the situation. One day I will get the three of us together for a night out – a geographic nightmare, I know!

Graham: for trusting me with your extensive collections and knowledge of them, thank you. I hope to convince you to tell your stories one day. Between us we could write something quite epic. I'm not going to give up on this, be warned. Oh, and just you mind my little buddie's blind-side!

Networking and marketing has become an important part of my life and I'd like to take this opportunity to thank my Twitter, Instagram and Facebook family. Not all of these platforms are about groups as such, yet there is a strong sense of community amongst us. To each and every one of you my sincere gratitude. To the group of us that have daily contact, the strength I gain from knowing I have your support is phenomenal.

Inspiration comes from many places. If your novel, biography or anthology has made it onto my website or if I have shared publicly that I'm enjoying your work then it's a heartfelt comment and I thank you that you've given me the motivation to fight on through my own journey. There are too many of you to mention – but you all know who you are.

DISCLAIMER — Throughout recent interviews Donna has discussed how writing is a process of therapy for her. Although she challenges many symptoms developed as a result of her head injury within writing The Warwick Cooper Thrillers, they remain works of fiction. In no way do the story-lines represent her life or lives of people she knows.

1

OBSESSION

Obsession is a dangerous condition. It's fair to say this case has a hold over me. As the original Detective Chief Inspector, you might say I am personally invested – solving it my priority. Pinned on the wall of my spare bedroom are the images of his crimes. They are as sickening as the first time I set eyes upon them; time does nothing to dampen the impact they have on me. To my left, his original victims. To my right, his more recent ones. My image appears on both sides.

The mutilated bodies of his earlier endeavours are a million miles from what he's done since his escape from prison last autumn. The change in his modus operandi so vivid but very obviously focused on revenge – revenge upon my team of detectives that had caught up with him. Mel Sage, Jen Jennings and I had been his intended targets last year and he didn't care who got in his way to reach us. As I gaze at the information before me I know we're missing something vital. His new victimology was screaming at me; I just had absolutely no idea what it was saying.

Deciding to run through the evidence once more today I stand back and contemplate what's before me on the wall. As much as I understand that he would hate the three of us for stopping him carrying out his fantasies, what he'd orchestrated was so very different to what he'd done in the past. Sam Cooper, my partner, and I had talked this through so many times. We couldn't put our finger on why he'd shift in the way he operated and it bothered me.

During the original crimes he was up close and personal. Fulfilling his perverse needs through his behaviours, rituals and sexual brutality. A sexual predator who targeted vulnerable women. Exploitation of their minds, bodies and souls was his pure enjoyment. The shift in him is a transformation I'm struggling to accept. Prison had created a new dimension to this monster. It appeared he'd taken a step back – he was letting others do his work. Including his murdering. Had he lost control of his gang while inside? Was this the difference we'd missed? Making a note on a new card I pinned this question onto the wall with the many others.

Arresting this man had put a price on my head. I'd escaped death three times since. The knife attack he orchestrated from his prison cell left me with extreme anxiety and despite having had treatment for that, it's something that remains. Until his escape last year, his responsibility for this had been kept from me – A member of his gang had forced Sam and I into an empty railway station where a second man waited with a knife. He'd plunged it into my back.

Sam held his hands into my bleeding wound until help arrived and stayed at the hospital until he knew I'd survived. I lost a kidney that night, resulting in some life-changing decisions: moving from the city I'd loved so much, my job and from the man I could no longer watch with another woman. I moved to

Polperro in Cornwall to begin a new chapter in my life.

His persistence in attempting to kill me didn't sit easily with me. After he'd blown up a train I was supposed to have been travelling on, but had missed by seconds, I knew I needed to keep looking over my shoulder. The feelings of guilt that this bomb was for me but had killed so many people while I lay in the arms of my lover is immense. His third attempt had drastic consequences. Sam and I were taking Charlie, Sam's son, to Scotland where he would begin training to work with Kerry. We were involved in a car chase that lasted for hours. Rain fell heavily in the Scottish Highlands that night and we hit something in the road. As our car flipped over, end to end, all three of us thought it was over. It was for Charlie. Sam lost his son that night, thanks to the psychopath we have become so involved with. While Sam and I lay unconscious in the dark, Charlie's body was removed from the car and tied to a tree and shot several times. An ace of spades playing card was placed in his mouth.

Escaping death three times takes its toll.

My two friends and ex colleagues, Jen Jennings and Mel Sage, had their lives changed on the night Ashbeck escaped from prison too. Jen, the victim of a car crash that he had ordered is now confined to a wheelchair. Her movement is slowly returning but still limited. Mel's trauma was horrific; having been kidnapped, held captive in a filthy cellar, gang raped, mutilated and crudely tattooed. Physical injuries aside the psychological impact on her is astounding – understandably so.

Ashbeck's attacks on my team bothered me for many reasons aside them not fitting within the victimology we were familiar with from his past. He'd manipulated influential pillars of society from inside his prison cell who had helped him escape. Included among these names was Max Smith, the Deputy Commissioner of London's metropolitan police force; the family man with a good reputation for making the streets of our city a safer place. Smith, still missing, hadn't taken much persuasion to rush to assist a psychopath.

We needed to establish what hold this man had over such men and Smith's youngest daughter handed us the answer. She was protecting his journal when armed response broke down the door to his family home to rescue the rest of the Smith family who had been held hostage there. The journal had proven rather revealing.

Smith wasn't alone. Phil Andrews, boss to myself and Sam but also a trusted friend, had fallen foul of his charms. Involved at such a deep level at the time of his escape last Autumn, Phil had taken his own life on the beach in Great Yarmouth in front of us. The sound and image of which neither Sam or I will ever be able to erase from our memories.

Sam wasn't involved in the original case, but he'd outranked me when we went undercover last year. Neither of us worked for the London's metropolitan police service any longer – instead a formidable woman called Kerry Preston employed us at her private investigation company. Kerry answers directly to the Home Office. Sam and I had become equals both at work and in the bedroom – we make a formidable team.

All public sightings of this man had resulted in negative

results for us so far. Sam was, it seemed, forever chasing up the latest ones. It concerned me that I'd not heard from him in a few days and I make a mental note to call him later.

The concept causing me the most anxiety was the notion that bodies would start turning up. That he would start killing again. The thought chills me to my bones.

I'd looked into the soul of Carl Ashbeck, and never really recovered.

2

HOME COMING

Darkness is her preferred time. She felt she could be herself when nobody else could see her, learning long ago to move under the cover of the shadows – something she did with ease these days. Shadow was the name she'd chosen when he'd asked.

For now, she sat at the kitchen table in the house she once called home. Having used her backdoor key to let herself in, she now contemplated her next move. Inhaling deeply through her nose she allowed the familiar fragrance to penetrate her senses as the oilcloth glided over the barrel of her handgun. Closing her eyes, she tried to envisage how this was going to play out.

They wouldn't recognise her, not to begin with. She'd lost five stone in weight since they'd last bothered to visit. Gone were the bold flowery dresses her mother had insisted she wore: instead black leathers graced her slender, athletic, toned body. At thirty-one she wasn't going to take their nonsense any longer.

It was time.

Stashing the oilcloth into the bag she'd dumped on the table as she stood, Shadow made her way from the kitchen towards the lounge. Making no attempt to disguise the sound of her high heeled ankle boots as they clicked on the wooden floor because the television was turned up loudly – her father, apparently, still refusing to wear his hearing aid. Despite the lack of lighting she knew there were no photos of her or her older sister among the family portraits on the walls or the console table. That wouldn't matter soon enough: the images that would remain embedded in her memory would be of her making.

Pausing briefly for composure, she takes a steadying breath before bringing her gun to eye level. Slowly emerging around the corner of the opened door waiting patiently until they notice, watching. Her parents, side by side on the sofa, are fully engaged in whatever it was they're watching. Shadow stands, smirking waiting for them to realise they have company, which takes a full minute, and she wishes she could video the moment they realise their fate. That way, she could relish this moment whenever it pleased her, but it's too risky.

Suddenly alert, eyes wide with fear, they reach for each other and hold hands – gripping so tightly, their knuckles turn white: bewilderment and a sense of knowing settling over them, as she begins to speak.

"Bet you didn't expect to see me tonight!"

Deep down they knew what would become of them if their youngest daughter ever came home and tonight their worst nightmare was forming in front of their eyes. She had appeared from nowhere and was now pointing a gun towards their heads. Her mother, begging for their lives, begins to plea. As yet her father sits in silence.

"Darling, why don't you put down the gun?" the ageing

woman says with a shaky voice.

"Not likely, mother. For the record, after that night I knew you'd have been a different person without his influence but that never changed the fact you turned the other way for so many years. When you visited me on your own, you were warmer towards me."

"Darling, that's a little harsh, don't you think. All your father has ever wanted was the best for you."

"The best? All that jerk ever wanted was for me to carry out what he didn't have the balls to do for himself. I was a child forced to carry out unthinkable tasks and you told my teachers on numerous parent's evenings that you had no idea why I wasn't developing normal social skills. Well fuck you!" She almost spat the words before turning her venom to her father. "You had me," she pauses, not wanting to say it aloud. "covering up your mess" and back at her mother, "and you turned a blind eye."

Pausing momentarily, she takes a steadying breath.

"I was eight years old when it all started for me. That fucks with my mind."

Firing a single shot that reverberates through the house, Shadow hits her mother between the eyes. Slumping backwards the woman goes limp and falls away from her husband. Her fingers uncurling, with his refusing to let go.

Turning her attention to her father, she sneers at him. She'd love to spend time, taunting him, but she can't afford to. Emotion can't get the better of her. With a cold heart, she fires the gun a second time, another perfect hit between the eyes. Watching as he slumps over his dead wife she smiles and takes four steps into the room. Reaching inside her breast pocket in her jacket, she pulls an item from it. Tearing it in half, she places it on the coffee table.

Her signature.

Briefly, a moment of sadness touches her heart for her mother, but it passes almost instantly. No tears form for she has no choice, there can be no other way. Her mission was clear. Once she'd shared the horrors within this house, the ghosts of her past, Ashbeck had demanded she takes control.

And she would do anything for him.

Somewhere in the house she knows there will be foster children: from what her mother had told her, at least two. Retreating from the lounge she makes her way towards the stairs. Again, her heels sounding on the wooden floor, her hands now trembling slightly.

Pausing before beginning her ascent a cold shiver runs the length of her spine and her heart begins to thump in her chest. Memories begin to flood her conscious thoughts – the sound of a shovel moving soil and the feeling of cold, disembodied dead flesh as she hides what he's done. What he's made her be part of. A childhood lost to a monster she called dad, to a mother who looked the other way, and a sister who ran away from home at fourteen.

Feeling nauseous she presses on, for there is a mission to complete. The more steps she climbs, the more her hands shake. A flooding of a different memory – her lost innocence and the baby she never got to know.

She needs to gather herself.

Anger begins to spike within her as she hesitates outside what used to be her own bedroom. Holding the gun in front of her body and composing herself with each controlled breath she regains focus. When she feels ready, with her fingers wrapping around the door handle and pressing gently upon it, the door opens.

Scanning the room, panic sets in at the sight of the empty bunk. Covers in disarray, whoever had occupied it gone. Readjusting her focus on the top bunk she aims the gun at the young child asleep there and fires one shot between her young eyes. Glancing around the room and under the bed she can't see any signs of another child. Removing a second item from her top pocket, Shadow tears it in half and places it near the body.

Having been told there was a male child in the house she headed along the landing to her sister's old room. She'd special instructions for him. As she enters the lad is stirring, already rubbing his eyes and trying to focus in the dark. Before he knows what is happening a pool of blood is seeping into the pillow beneath his head.

Her next move, a direct order from Ashbeck, is callous even to her. Without hesitation, or emotion she carries out her order and doesn't leave until she's removed a third item from her top pocket, torn it in half and placed it near the body.

Moving swiftly through the house, retracing her steps back to the kitchen she collects her bag and exits through the back door. As an afterthought she places the key from the worktop into the lock, closes the door and smashes the glass to make it look like a break-in.

Making her way along the pathway she places her helmet over her head, fastens it and takes her keys from her pocket. By the time she reaches her motorbike, her bag is secured on her back and she's ready to ride. The BMW S 1000 RR roars into life. Ensuring to keep the revs to a minimum to avoid disturbing the neighbours, Shadow rides off into the night. The last thing she needed was for the locals to start curtain twitching, and it was that sort of neighbourhood.

3

BABY TRADE

Nineteen-eighty-seven.

The radio played quietly, almost inaudibly, as they park outside the red brick building. Dressed in black the couple moved quickly. They had a specific mission to complete; perhaps an unethical one depending upon your perception of the matter. The order had arrived three hours ago from concerned grandparents. A child removal was required. Payment had been by cash to the collector. The deal made. Two sisters, one four years old and a new born baby.

The hospital was just as it had been described. A grand red brick Victorian building that had seen better days; a workhouse back in the day, but that wasn't their concern.

The family they were interested in at this location had been separated from the rest. All the other new mothers were in a ward together. This family wouldn't be taking their new-born home, they'd been told it had died during delivery by members of their own family for it was safer for the infant. This had been agreed by the midwife, who'd accepted an envelope of money – she only had to look at the older child to know the old man's reasons.

All the babies were either tucked up in their transparent cribs or nestling with their mothers – except one.

One was in the arms of her grandfather who had stolen her from the nursery and sneaked her into the corridor at the agreed time. His heart surged as a mix of anxiety and anticipation seeped through his body, unsure if he'd made the right decision. A little girl stood, clinging to the hem of his jacket – her face bruised from the latest beating. Standing with the only person with whom she felt secure, about to be abandoned.

Moving along the scarcely lit corridor the couple move swiftly, closing in on this sad sight. A family about to be separated for good. The smell of disinfectant filled the air and stung the back of their throats. They'd had instruction on the precise location and within thirty seconds of entering had turned around with the two children in their possession. Silent tears cascaded down the old man's cheeks as he watched his two grandchildren disappear from his life for good. The couple exit through the same door they entered, turned the corner and bundled the children into the waiting car before driving away quickly and without fuss.

The young child, void of emotion sat in the back and the infant in the arms of the woman, swaddled and content. They travelled in silence.

New to the area, the couple hadn't realised how close to the hospital they lived. The drive had only taken twenty minutes. Concerned by this, he had no choice but to push it to the back of his mind and place his efforts on the decision he knew he had to make next. From the look on his wife's face he knew these girls weren't going anywhere. The pair of them had tried to conceive for a child for many years without success and now she'd bonded with the baby – it had taken her twenty minutes.

Business contacts still had to be met, however. Money had already been exchanged, yet he no longer had the merchandise to hand over. Forging a new plan, he arrived at the agreed rendezvous first. Will Collins was ready and waiting. He'd chosen a woodland area, remote and away from passing traffic. When, eventually, a car approached he flashed his headlight beam once, which was reciprocated. Entering new territory now, he stepped out of his car and waited beside it. Feeling the weight of the pistol in his right pocket, and unsure how this was going to work – but knowing he had to do something.

The couple stopped, stepped out of their car and started to walk towards him. Their smiles and body language expectant at the prospect of meeting their new family for the first time. Letting them get as close as he dared, he smiled back. Reaching into his right pocket he felt for the hand grip and released the safety catch before bringing the gun out into full view. Taking aim and without hesitation he gently squeezes the trigger twice in quick succession, watching as the couple collapse just a few metres from his feet.

Without delay he pops the boot of his car and arranges the plastic within it. Carrying the first body, the man, he lays him inside the boot before fetching the woman and placing her with him. He then removes his jacket and lays it over them, before wrapping the plastic over the lot and slamming the boot closed. Sliding back behind the wheel and firing the engine he pulls away from the cover of the trees onto the road, towards home.

Moving to the new property had been stressful enough but tonight's change in tactics topped that. Nothing could have prepared his mind, or body, for the stress he endured during the drive home with two bodies in the boot. With sweaty palms and a palpitating heart, he pressed on fearful that every headlight was the police looking for him. Paranoia seeping in, justifiable. Wondering if his wife would understand his bold move and needing her compliance if all this was to work out. After all, it was because of her needs – her desire to have a child – they were in this position. They needed each other more than ever now.

The sound of a shovel scraping away at dirt came through the crack in the cellar door. At four years old, Kay was too inquisitive for her own good. Peeping through she leant against the door and it moved, giving out a loud creak.

The new person she'd been told to call dad encouraged her down further and handed her a trowel. Together they moved soil until a massive hole in the ground was before them. They'd been working away since early afternoon. Tired, hungry and thirsty, she'd asked to leave but he wouldn't let her go. Instead, he moved her towards a dark corner and rustled something she'd not noticed. As she moved closer and her eyes started adjusting in the darkness, the sight before her became confusing. The smell made her tummy churn and she was almost sick. What lay at her feet horrible but somehow mesmerising.

The look in his eyes instilled a fear within her and she forced the burning liquid back down her throat, making her eyes water. Despite tired and uncooperative muscles, from the digging, he forced her to take an arm and help him carry the dead woman.

Transfixed to the soulless eyes that watched her, she did as she was asked. Once at the edge of the hole, she watched as the body rolled over the edge and dropped to the bottom. This monster of a man took her by the hand and pulled her back into the dark corner, when the process was repeated for the second body – a man. Again, transfixed by the eyes, she was forced to take an arm and help him move it to the edge of the hole. Horrified, she watched as the man rolled over the edge to join the first body at the bottom of the hole.

"We never speak of this, ever. Do you understand?"

Nodding as she runs towards the steps, where her tired flimsy legs struggle to clamber to the top, she squeezes herself through the gap in the doorway and narrowly avoids the arms of the woman, she now calls mum, the other side who's waiting for her. Still running she heads for the wooden stairs and into her new bedroom, where she buries her head into her pillow to cry herself to sleep – the smell of dirt and dead bodies lingering in her nostrils and on her body.

Having been removed from one hell, she'd been placed some place far worse. Her involvement immediate in helping her new father dispose of his evidence and, eventually, protecting her sister as best she could.

There was no choice, no explanation, no escape.

Several years passed before the younger child became involved in his game. She was good. Better than the older one. His favourite. Kay had tried to prevent it, but he was too persuasive. There was no point staying after that.

4

SHADOW

Shadow only had to close her eyes to hear it: the sound of the shovel scraping at gravel in the basement and to remember how the dirt beneath her fingernails felt, the dryness it left behind on her skin and how it all smelt. She only had to close her eyes to revisit the isolation she felt of being in his cellar: of preparing another grave for him while he went about his business. The man who was supposed to protect her. Her father: the man who relied on his child to cover up for him. Always finding fault in all that she did, no matter how hard she worked for him.

Hating what he'd made her do with a passion, she would sneak back down here when she thought everyone else was sleeping to kneel at each grave and to pray for each of the victims. Once she was finished, she'd shed a tear, before standing and plunging something sharp into her own flesh, her blood dripping onto the soil beneath her feet, releasing the pressure that built within her each day: giving part of herself to his victims for what he made her do in whatever sick game he was into. For just these few moments every day it made her feel better, giving her back some control. That was all she had.

Snapping her mind back to reality, Shadow had just watched headlights drawing closer in her rear-view mirror. Checking her speed, she eased on the throttle in case it was a patrol car. At worse, they'd pull her over for inappropriate footwear. Always a risk to wear high heeled boots riding her bike, she knew but it made her feel phenomenal. More of a worry at times like this were the concealed weapons she carried. Not only was her gun tucked away on the inside of her jacket, but her knife was always to hand. It was safely sheathed in the especially designed hand-crafted leather pouch on the inside of her left boot. Lucky to be ambidextrous she preferred to use her gun with her right hand but had learnt, with great efficiency, to use a knife with her left. Not even her job with her sister would give her an excuse to carry a weapon.

Closing in fast, the car was weaving between the other vehicles on the duel carriageway. Great. Paranoia fast taking over when it pulled in behind her, slowing in order to follow, its blue light sitting proudly upon the roof. Seven minutes passed before it had seen enough, and the driver pulled around her and sped off.

Deciding to take the next exit and a country detour towards her sister's house, Shadow refocused her mind. The junction wasn't far ahead but she'd need to keep an eye out for it. Badly sign-posted, for the small villages didn't want an influx of large vehicles passing through.

Taking the slip road, she was pleased to leave the monotony

of riding in traffic behind. Opening the throttle, she intended to enjoy the freedom of this country lane – knowing how quiet it would be at this late hour. Finally feeling more relaxed she begins to negotiate cambers the only way she knew how: with the precision of a professional rider. It wasn't until she'd sped past the layby and the police car that was sat within it that her panic set in once again.

Opening the throttle further, the chase was on. Knowing the road well she could only pray she didn't meet any vehicles head-on. If she could out-ride the car for half a mile without any hold-up there was a track off to the left she could use. The joy of this bike is its just as efficient off-road as it is on the tarmac.

As the track neared, she braked and turned before opening the throttle again. Now cursing her choice of footwear for the task, she started to negotiate the easy part of the track. This section of forest was firm under her tyres and the car wasn't far behind in its pursuit. Gradually, as the track narrowed, and mud started to flick out behind the bike she knew the car would struggle. The terrain became trickier from here and the car would soon have to stop. She knew they would have radioed for backup and she had two options: to carry on through the woodland and hope the gate was open the other end, but there was no guarantee of that; or make a right turn shortly which would bring her back out on the road she'd just left but half a mile along.

Deciding to turn right, she took the opportunity to glance behind her and was startled to see the car still in pursuit. Smiling to herself, as she knew it wouldn't be able to turn around, she continued on her way as the track narrowed and was almost impassable in places.

Without a second glance behind her, she pressed on. When her tyres hit tarmac a few minutes later, mud splattered along the road for two hundred metres. She'd lost the police car but knew she needed to get off this road quickly. Back-up would have been dispatched and there was always the possibility of a helicopter. She couldn't take any chances.

Her sister's house was only five minutes away. That was five minutes too far in her eyes. Despite not having had plans to visit, they'd just changed. Whatever her story, she'd trust her, she had to. Not only were they sisters, but they were bonded in another way too. They worked together.

Her second job gave high financial reward, but it was the connection she had with him that was of importance to her. He was the only person who seemed to understand and had taken the time to listen, to care and it was him who had wanted to seek revenge and help her gain closure. Despite her sister having lived through similar experiences she'd closed down this part of her life.

It was because of him, that she needed to carry the gun. That she had learnt with great skill to use it efficiently. He'd been a good teacher and his military background had helped with that. He had taught her how to deal with the impact of killing someone, how to dismiss it and how to become cold towards death. How not to feel. She'd needed to learn that. Because of him she now coped with her past and what her father had made her do. She owed him everything.

Facing her sister wouldn't be easy. She would, by now, know that their parents were dead. She would suspect her, of that she was certain and knows her well enough to realise that she'd have set up a private search on her to establish her whereabouts at the very least. There would be gaps in her movements that she couldn't explain and that wouldn't be welcomed.

London is her playground now. Her whole life has been about conformity, relinquishing control to others but that doesn't happen anymore. As darkness follows light, so a shadow falls over the soul of this woman. The good she has done for one organisation far outweighed by the work she's done for the other.

An inner hatred for the abandonment she felt at being left behind in a house of horrors, to bury corpses for their father and with a mother who looked the other way, took its toll and this drives her needs.

The complexities of her situation gave her the opportunity to regain control by providing her prospects. Her contact in the dark world she inhabits understands her. When he first reached out she thought she'd be doing the right thing and would hand the information over to the correct people. That his associates would be arrested. When they met, however she helped him in ways she thought she'd never be entangled in: they clicked, and she became a double agent. No one suspects her. It has been easy. With all the resources at her fingertips, and the generosity of both bosses being eternally grateful to remain a step or two ahead of the game she fed them enough from each side. Both expected and rewarded loyalty but only he knew the truth. Over the years his loyalty had resulted in friendship and trust. She'd become his protector. Ultimately, if anything happened to him, she would be the one to inherit.

Owning and living above her London bar, she'd made some special conversions to the building. The cellar, in particular contains special features. Soundproofing was the first and most important addition, her priority. Heavy duty rings were added to the walls, with chains and arm cuffs. At times she had to handle four prisoners at once and could not have them gang up on her, so they were adequately spaced apart. Often alone, she learnt early on to keep her distance when dealing with them. There had been a couple of times where she had compromised her safety – wandering too close. She'd been grabbed once and that had been her wake-up call. Gang members, awaiting persecution were kept here until he arrived. It was never pretty, and she liked to watch. He was a cruel man from whom she'd learnt so much.

5

DEVRON'S GILLIE

Approximately seven hundred miles away April Parmenter stands on flint, reaching up to peep through the window of a wooden hut that sat alongside the River Devron. Surprised to see a log burner ablaze in the corner to her left but now realising why she'd seen the stream of smoke trailing into the sky as she'd approached. A large pine table dominated the room. Arranged on top were tea-light candles on an emptied out one-use BBQ kit, a folder and an assortment of pens. Posters identifying types of salmon fish and a notice board adorned the walls.

As beautiful as she found the surrounding countryside, February was bitterly cold in Netherdale, a remote location in Aberdeenshire. Temptation to try the hut door, to be warmed by the fire was rather overwhelming. Thinking she'd appreciate just ten minutes of warmth before she continued her walk.

The hut, she knew, was a gillie hut and that a gillie was someone who monitored fishing along the river. She'd never met a gillie as best she knew. The hut sat just back from the pathway that ran alongside the water's edge at an angle with a farm track that ascended the valley. Parked at an angle, between the track and the hut she'd noticed a white four-wheel drive truck, its wheel-arches packed out with mud. Mud splashes obliterated much of the sides of the vehicle, covering most of the paintwork.

Panic takes over; the sound of birds chirping and the river running over rocks fades into the distance, replaced by footsteps on the stones behind her. Taking a deep breath, she steadies her nerves and braces herself. Feeling a braveness from someplace deep within she attempts to turn around. Something doesn't feel right. The presence behind her too close, making the hairs on her arms stand to attention as terror engulfs every cell in her body.

No one has spoken yet, unnerving her further. The need to run suddenly overpowering, her legs primed like coiled springs as she prepares herself to escape. Spinning her body round, she suddenly feels hot breath on her neck and an arm clenching at her throat. Choking and panicked, her eyes wide and blood pounding in her ears she flails her arms in an attempt at freeing herself: the harder she tries the tighter the hold becomes. The grip around her neck slowly starving her of air as she tries her hardest to gasp.

With the sound of blood pumping in her ears, April's eyes roll as blackness overcomes her.

Allowing her to fall into his arms, he scoops her up easily as if she's a small child and carries her around the front of the hut, onto the decked area. Back-kicking the door, it swings open. Greeted by the crackling and warmth of the wood burner – always welcoming in his view – he entered and laid her limp body on the table.

Four minutes it should have taken for the blood flow to have been restricted to her brain, yet it had been far less. She was weak. Or he'd been too brutal. Hoping she wasn't dead, he begins CPR to bring her back into this world. Learning long ago that it was no use knowing the blood choke technique without knowing how to bring a person round again. He wanted and needed her alive. There'd be no fun if she was dead, for something new and exciting was planned.

Having snuck into a house earlier he'd not believed his luck. On the kitchen counter had sat a huge knife, sheathed in a leather case. It was beautiful. Heavy. The black leather casing embossed with a deer and an ear of corn. Removing the blade, he'd been thrilled at the sight and it was newly sharpened too. The feel of it now, tucked inside the top of his right boot; empowering.

True to most fishermen, he carried reels of fishing line in the back of his vehicle. Right now, he had one in his back pocket. Removing it, he unravels a couple of metres. Unsheathing the knife, he cuts it. Although one strand isn't very strong, once it is wound over and over it is more than sufficient to bind a person. Holding her wrists together, he binds them and ties a knot then repeats the process for her ankles. All the time he tries to not look at her face. Her pleading eyes not helping him as he thinks about the impact this will have on his family if he gets caught. Needing to secure her onto the table he passes the line over the body and under the table, over and over, making sure to tie a knot when he was done.

Convinced no one would venture here at this time of the day at this time of year, he was willing to leave the woman for a short while but was cautious. Despite the hut normally being unlocked he couldn't risk someone stumbling on his catch of the day. Making sure he locks the door before jumping in his four-wheel drive, he heads towards home. The track, streaked with water, made the start of his journey sluggish but he loved the sound of his tyres as they passed over the mud mixed with rock as they travelled over it. Dirty water splashed up the side of his vehicle, the sound relaxing him and calming his anxiety. He needed that right now.

His wife would expect him home in twenty minutes, he mustn't be late. Lateness would result in a stream of questions that he didn't need tonight. What he needed was to eat his dinner in silence, like they usually did.

Having bolted his dinner faster than normal, Matt Collins was out the door before his wife could question him. He couldn't believe he'd left the woman in the hut, unattended. That was chancy. Speeding along the narrow lanes towards the scene, to the reward that awaited him, sent a surge of adrenaline through his body. The more he thought about his plans the more intense the throbbing between his legs became. This response surprised him but was welcome.

Taking less time than usual to reach the track he slowed to negotiate the mud. Heavy rain started to fall as he did, which was fine for now but if it continued like this he'd need to be careful later. Arriving, he spins the truck around so he's facing the right direction for a hasty exit. Leaving the engine running he leaps out, slamming the truck door shut. With a pounding heart he rummages in his pocket for the keys and runs towards the door, startled at how difficult it is to move quickly with an erection fighting against his jeans. Fumbling with the key, his hand trembles as he attempts to unlock the door. Seconds take an eternity as this simple task drives frustrations he wasn't expecting. As the door releases he bursts through the gap, his eyes wild with desire, his pupils dilated as if in a drug-like state.

Slamming the door behind him, Matt moves up close to the woman. With fear in her eyes, she looks at him with hope he'll show mercy. Removing the knife from his right boot he takes it from its leather sheath, slowly and deliberately; the blade glistening in the light of the fire as he twists the blade in his hand. He runs his finger along it, smiling at her. Saliva escapes from the corner of his mouth, swiping it with his arm, he wipes it with his cuff. His smile turns into a cruel snarl as he drops his gaze to her ankles and swipes at the binds with the knife.

"No!" April begs, taking a sharp intake of breath. "Please don't, I beg you." She says as she starts to struggle.

Prising her legs apart, he throws himself over her and holds the knife against her throat. Suddenly motionless, fear freezes her into submission. A dark patch appears between her legs as her bladder empties and urine soaks into denim.

Uninterested in her body, he straddles her and immediately sets to work. The blade, contacting skin, sends a trickle of blood into her hair that seeps onto the table below her, pooling. Taking his time, he gradually begins removing what he needs. The louder she screams the harder he becomes and the faster the blood pools beneath her. He continues to slice away.

April, suddenly quiet gives in to shock and unconsciousness becomes her. He has a little more work to do before he's finished. Careful not to nick the precious trophy he swaps to a smaller blade. The scalpel he'd been instructed to use – this mask was needed for something special, apparently.

Placing his trophy into a specially designed box, he places it on the table before wiping his blades on a cloth hanging from a back pocket. Returning his new knife to its leather sheath, he tucked it back into his right boot. The scalpel went in the bin in the corner, un-phased about DNA or fingerprints.

After hours of thought there was no grand plan of how to dispose of the body. His brother had been successful at that, none of his bodies had ever been found. Since his death, however the murder orders had begun filtering through to him which hadn't sat comfortably. This woman had been his first, and he'd enjoyed the experience. Never had he felt so aroused – his erection still throbbing beneath his jeans.

He'd made a rushed decision about this body. It would be discovered. Having wedged the door open he moves back to the woman and lifts her. Still warm, she is limp in his arms as he carries her into the cold air, blood dripping from her body leaving a trail. Darkness is suffocating as he carries her towards the river. Mindful of his step he places the lifeless body on the river's edge and takes his time to arrange her correctly. He wants her just so. He has it in his mind, how he wants her found.

His first. His angel.

Hanging his jacket on the hooks above the wood burner to dry, he sets to work on clearing up. Removing the parts of her that had been ordered had proven messy. Shocked there was a market for such macabre merchandise but willing to provide for the handsome price he'd received. The risk was nothing for that. Unlike his brother there was no cellar, for now. This needed to change. Two more jobs of this calibre would provide the funds he needed. In the mean-time his bodies would be found but he'd make sure that each killing would be different – that they couldn't be linked to each other.

Having picked up the metal bucket from the corner he ventured back to the river's edge and scooped water from it. Returning to the wood burner, he places it on top to heat. Always disinfectant to hand for cleaning canoes and fishing equipment he uses what he has to set about the cleaning process.

Astounded at the quantity of blood one body produced – he knew one bucket of water wouldn't be enough. He'd hoped that the hut would suffice for each of his killings, but the blood had soaked into the wooden floor. The reality of having to find more locations, gradually dawning on him as the gravity of what he was doing impacts upon him. His next hit was in seven days. Finding a new location was a priority. He wasn't even sure forensics would be finished with this place by then, anyhow.

The rain was relentless, gaining momentum, pounding on the hut roof. The sound echoed with the crackling fire. He was thankful for the warmth this was providing as he continued to scrub blood from the table top. This process somehow spreading a contentment through him, relaxing his anxiety. He'd been emotionally edgy all evening and looking back it shocked him at how turned on he'd been throughout the process. Perhaps he'd be able to rekindle a closeness with his wife now – perhaps it was too late for that. It was worth a try.

With his thoughts unable to remain focused, his brother now materialised within them. Uncertainty of who or why he and his wife were murdered bothered him somewhat. The oldest daughter had worried the family for many years with her choice of career – she had remained loyal however and hadn't ever revealed the family's dark secret. The younger one was a ticking time-bomb. He'd be forever looking over his shoulder for her. Contacts had informed him that she was involved in an influential gang in London as well as working for her sister: a dangerous woman. A double agent.

6

COLD STEEL

Sam Cooper always leaves his bedroom door ajar these days, the light from the hallway seeping through. It certainly makes him feel better about going to bed. Despite his dislike of guns within civilian life, there's one tucked under his pillow right now. No one knows – not even Kate because she no longer stays over.

Every night it happens: the flashback. Sam's body is soaked in sweat as his mind returns to the night of the accident: driving through a stormy night with Kate by his side and his only child, Charlie, in the back. Rain drives hard against the windscreen and onto the road. Water flows in torrents beneath them. Safer, perhaps to pull over and stop if it wasn't for the escaped prisoner chasing them in the car behind.

Carl Ashbeck had been tracking them for hours, bumper-to-bumper. Eventually they hit something in the road that caused the car to flip several times. Metal crunched against tarmac and the world begun to spin out of control as disorientation and flashes of light were replaced with darkness.

The emotional turmoil at seeing his son on a morgue gurney:

cold, naked, lifeless. Shot despite having already been dead, too much for Sam to cope with. Flashbacks are nightly. Haunting. The accident itself not as bad as what he'd woken to. The sound of gunshots had echoed through the trees, and then he had slipped back into unconsciousness.

The message was clear. A message of promised torture for him delivered on the body of his own son: wounds in each foot, each knee cap, each hand and each elbow and one between the eyes. Protruding from his mouth had been the ace of spades playing card.

Ashbeck's signature.

When Sam's mobile phone breaks the silence he automatically reaches for the cold steel and is suddenly bolt upright. Sweat beads roll down his forehead and over his face and his heart pounds. With laboured breathing he listens for sounds from beyond the room. It takes a few moments before he realises what has woken him.

"It's my day off," he grumbles into the phone "ruin it at your peril." Listening before responding "Christ! Give me a couple of minutes."

Getting out of bed Sam fumbles about collecting last night's clothes and giving them a smell. Sneering he throws them to the floor. Moving to his wardrobe he stashes the handgun in his safe and secures the door before selecting clean clothes. He retreats to his bathroom to splash cold water on his face and upper body, to clean his teeth and throw his clothes on.

All the time he speaks into his mobile.

"Okay, but you'll have to swing by and pick me up. No way I'm driving."

Sam ends the call, smells his armpits and decides to run the hot water.

When Sam Cooper finally exits onto the street, shirt still unbuttoned, I'm already waiting for him in my black BMW. I tap my right hand on the steering wheel as heavy rock music plays loudly.

As he slams the passenger door shut, Sam hits the CD player to silence it, a scowl already formed on his face.

"You look like shit, Sam"

"What do you expect? Its my day off, whatever we're going to won't be a walk in the park."

He has a point.

Leaning back in the seat he buttons his shirt and I pull into the road. Traffic is quiet at this ridiculously early hour.

"What do we know?" He asks.

"Okay, the house belongs to Will and Jane Collins. They have three kids, all fostered. Both adults and two of the youngsters have been shot in the head. The youngest is missing. We think she's five."

Suddenly alert Sam slaps the dashboard with both hands, anger emitting from his eyes. A frown appears, forming deep burrows between his eyes and he twists in his seat turning to face me. I have his full attention.

"Shit! I hate it when it's kids! Why us? Why has Kerry sent us to this one?"

"I don't know. Not yet, anyhow."

The drive takes about an hour and a half. As we approach the scene, the country lane is narrow and trees arch overhead like a tunnel. Bright lights flash between bare branches, denoting that we are getting close. The sun was beginning to rise and frost had formed on the grass verges, glistening in the beams of the headlights.

A road block had been set up ahead and as we drew close I eased the car to a standstill. Pressing a button my electric window jumps into life as it lowers to let in a blast of February air. The male officer walks towards us, a stern look on his face. As he arrives, he leans in the car, probably appreciative of a moment's warmth on his face. When he speaks the garlic on his breath is overpowering.

"Morning. I'm afraid you'll have to turn around. This roadblock will be in place most of the day." He announces.

"Good morning. You should be expecting us." I chirp as I produce our credentials and hand them over to him, allowing him time to absorb the information.

This would go one of two ways. Kerry Preston, our boss, would have phoned ahead and informed the local police force of our required involvement in this case. This would be accepted, or we would have to fight our way in. Time would tell but we would not allow ourselves to be turned away. Our presence here could only mean one thing. That Carl Ashbeck had a link to this crime, however direct or indirect.

"Yeah, we're expecting you. Don't use the driveway. Park up the road on the left, it will be obvious. Neighbours reported a motorbike leaving so we're waiting for daylight before we can search properly. We've cordoned off a walkway." He moves off and walks towards the cones in the road, moving them out of our way.

Returning the window into its gap, grateful for the last moments of warm air before we enter the cold morning and whatever horrors we'll face within this house. Once parked I take a moment to check on Sam.

"You okay?"

"Yup."

"Kerry asked me to leave you at home this morning. I need your word you can handle this. Look me in the eyes and tell me you're on top form today."

Reluctantly, he gives me his eyes. My heart softens as it always does when I become lost within such moments. Ashbeck had ruined our chances and now Sam was in too deep. For him, this case had become too personal.

"No Kate, I'm not on top form but I'm here and I need to be a part of this. I've got bad attitude, bad breath, B.O. and a hangover."

"Don't forget the anger issues!" I say, smiling and holding out my hand, which he takes in his.

"Let's do this," I say, squeezing his hand.

Walking towards the tape at the property boundary we are faced with another officer. After producing our credentials a second time we obtain clearance.

"That's Frank Jones over there. He used to work at Paddington about two years before you and I became partners."

"You guys got on okay?"

"Of course."

"Handy contact then."

"Hey, Frank!"

"Sam? What you doin' 'ere?"

"This case has links to something I'm up to my neck in. How the hell are you man?"

"Bloody good to see you, Sam!" Frank says, and then he remembers. He bows his head – Frank Jones cannot look Sam in the eyes.

"It's good to see you, Frank."

"Sam. Eerm. I, er..."

"I know, thanks." Sam says, and as he walks off, adds "we'll talk about that later."

Returning to his searching duties under the front window, Frank is shaking his head and mumbling to himself. Bending, he reaches for something on the ground and stashes it into an evidence bag.

Approaching, I cannot help but admire the building. Red brick, symmetrical, and backlit with modern halogen lighting. An imposing building that I couldn't put a date to right now. The heavy wooden door was wide open and, in its frame stood a large man. Again, we were going to need to show our credentials. I knew Sam was going to be awkward. I could feel it.

Within thirty seconds I was cleared entry into the house. It took Sam over five minutes of argument, defiance and ultimately, the conformity he knew was required of him. Despite my patient exterior Sam could tell by my body language that he was pushing it with me. Whatever was going on in his head and his life, this was not necessary nor was it professional.

Forensics were collecting fibres, dusting for fingerprints, taking measurements and labelling samples. The pathologist was already here, and I was relieved to see someone Sam and I both knew well, Jim Jordan Peterson – better known as JJ.

"Sam! Kate! Good morning to you both. Sam, how's the head this morning? Man, you had some last night!" JJ is laughing.

"Like you'd expect JJ. He has a sore one! How are you? Haven't seen you for so long."

"Well, that's actually a good thing for crime if you think about it."

"I guess so," I laugh.

"I'm very well. You're looking tired, Kate. I hope you're taking care of yourself."

"Long hours, that's all. Apart from that I'm..."

"What've we got apart from the obvious, JJ?" Sam interrupts.

"This isn't official until I've done what I do."

"Yeah, yeah, yeah, just give me something to start with. I won't hold you to ransom."

JJ positions himself beside his young assistant, who is collecting fibres from the man's body.

"We assume this to be Will Collins, but tests will confirm this," pointing to the wound between his eyes, JJ continues "I'd hazard a guess at 9mm, shot fired from the doorway." Moving to Jane Collins's body, he points to her wound which looks identical to me. "Again, I'd say same weapon, same distance. This looks like a professional hit." JJ looks at me and holds eye contact "Okay, there's two more upstairs. "Kate, I want you to take a look."

"JJ, you can't get rid of me that easily." Sam protests as he follows us out the lounge into the hallway.

JJ stops, turns to face him and in a low whisper begins to speak,

"Sam, as your friend, I'm requesting you don't follow us upstairs. You don't need to see this." He turns and continues to the staircase, Sam hot on his heels, a look of defiance on his face.

Having climbed the stairs in silence, JJ enters the furthest bedroom, with sorrow showing in his eyes. The bedroom is tidy, decorated in pinks and yellows and is now harshly lit with spotlights that have been added by the forensics team. My eyes are drawn to the bed, against the longest wall, the bottom bed is empty.

A technician lifts the sheet that covers the body and hands it to JJ, who gently places it at the end of the bed, then looks at me with deep concern on his face. Hardly believing what's before me, I turn to Sam and watch the colour drain from his cheeks – wondering if he might faint. I have no words.

"This young lad, I believe, was awake. His eyes were open. The other child, a girl I believe was asleep."

"He did this to the girl too?" I ask.

"No, just to this lad."

Sam remained silent, staring and stunned. Sickened to the stomach to see identical gunshot wounds to those of his dead son. We were in no doubt as to why we were involved.

Ashbeck had to have been in this house because these details had not been released. There was one exceptional difference.

Moving along the landing we enter the second bedroom. Silence having fallen between us my initial thoughts remain my own for now. Something had gone wrong for the intruder in here. The bottom bunk was empty – covers pulled back in disarray but no body. Above, the top bunk displayed its horror.

A little girl of about eight years. It if wasn't for the wound between her eyes she would have been sleeping peacefully.

A female officer stood beside the bed – I nodded a greeting to her and she responded in kind.

The room looked like it had been ransacked and JJ had yet to speak a word. He'd left us to assess our surroundings, wanting our opinion.

"A penny for them?" He asks. "What are your first impressions, Kate?"

"Something went terribly wrong in here. There's a frightened little girl somewhere."

"Sam?"

"I hope to hell he's not kidnapped a little 'un!" He looks up at me, then at JJ. "I swear on Charlie's grave I'll tear the bastard apart myself!" He almost spits his words.

"Come on," I say, gently touching his arm and moving him towards the door: but something stops me. A noise.

"This is a grim scene. In all the years I've attended scenes, it's one of the worse…"

"Shush," I cut him off, "listen!" I whisper.

We hear the movement in unison, from somewhere behind the wooden panelling. I hold my hand up to silence everyone. We wait until there's more sound: shallow breaths from beyond the wall on the far side of the room are now evident. What sounds like fingernails scraping against wood suddenly fills the room and we all look at each other. Moving towards the sound, I squat.

"Hey, it's okay honey. My name's Kate and I'm a police officer." Of course this isn't strictly true but this frightened little girl, behind the wooden panelling, doesn't need to know the finer details.

"Why don't you come on out. It's safe now."

There was a shuffling noise as the hidden door squeaked and yielded. Breaking into my kindest smile I peep through the gap at frightened eyes – my whole body aching for this frightened girl.

"I'm going to open the door a little more for you, okay?"

As she nods I pull the door as wide as possible, gently stretching my arms towards her. She is four or five at most, and trembling. Scooping her into my arms I hold her frightened body to my own. She buries her head into my neck. I look up at Sam, his hand covers his mouth, his thumb massaging one cheek, his fingers the other. Turning my attention to JJ, I note a tear escape and tumble down his left cheek: a rare sight for him to see a survivor at a scene like this.

7

SILENCED

Normally great with children I wonder how Sam is doing: what place his mind must be in right now and if he was thinking about Charlie. He had to be thinking about Charlie.

I was thinking about Charlie.

Try as we might we had not been able to get this little girl to speak. An ambulance had been arranged and had now arrived; she needed to be taken to hospital to be checked over. Sam and I had been allocated to escort her because our work here had been completed. The ambulance crew caused a scene insisting that only one of us travel with them. Deciding to take the driver to one side, I have a quiet word.

"This little girl is a material witness and her life might well be in danger. Trust me, you need both of us for her protection and for the protection of you and your crew." I look him square in the eyes and refuse to break eye contact. I wasn't taking no for an answer.

"Okay." He said as he took air in through his teeth, making a whistling sound. Adding, "we don't get paid enough for this shit."

The two of us returned to the ambulance. Sam and the young girl were already aboard. She was strapped onto the stretcher and Sam in the seat near the rear doors. A paramedic was taking her blood pressure. I was invited into the front, with the driver.

There was no urgency to our journey. No sirens, no blue lights. No more drama needed. A relaxed drive for a trauamatised little girl who refused to give us her name. She knew ours and that had to be good enough for now.

Upon arrival at hospital we stayed close. There was a short delay during which paperwork transferred her from the care of one team to the next and for a cubicle to be found. Sam sat one side of her bed and me the other in a world that was silent for now. A kind nurse, Natalie, had bought her a hot chocolate and she was sitting up sipping at it – the colour returning to her cheeks. So far, she had shown no emotion – there was just a lost withdrawn look in her dark eyes. Eyes that had seen far too much for someone so young. For anyone, in all honesty.

Once she'd finished her drink, she passed her mug to Sam who placed it on the floor. She slid down under the blanket and smiled.

"Is there anything else you'd like?" Sam asked.

She shook her head.

Our first communication.

From beneath the blanket, a hand wiggled free and she held it out towards Sam. He took it into his own and allowed her to hold onto him. Progress. The silence had been deafening, but sudden life ignited in her eyes.

"My name is Jodie," she suddenly announces. "I'm five."

"Jodie? That's a pretty name and there's no way you are five. I thought you were nine!" Sam says with a large grin on his face.

"It's an ugly name. Daddy told me so."

My heart sinks. I can't help but wonder what this little girl had been through before being fostered. Jodie's life had already been traumatic, and she now found herself in the middle of whatever game Ashbeck had planned for her. Her young life had just become far more complex than she could comprehend.

Sam, forever prepared, glossed over her answer because we were not allowed to question her. Their banter continued, and I smiled as I watched.

"I'm never nine. You're silly!" She said through giggles. Sam was laughing too.

"Come on then, how old do you think I am?"

After a little thought,

"well older than me. Eerm, seventy!"

Sam's mouth dropped open and I laughed aloud.

"Seventy? I don't think so!" Placing his hands on his hips he raises both eyebrows at her, which makes her laugh. "And what about Kate over there, how old do you think she is?"

"Twenty-five." Jodie states without thinking, in a serious voice and with no hint of jollity.

Sam and I exchange looks, both of us having noted her change in attitude. Why would she be scared of me?

Sam needed coffee and I needed air. Volunteering to find a vending machine, I head out in search of both. Finding the outside first, I open the door to the welcome bitterness of the February afternoon and wrap my jacket around my body. A man already stands here, having snuck out in his hospital gown to smoke. Taking his first deep draw on his cigarette as he savoured his addiction, he turns and smiles at me. Knowing he's every intention to strike conversation, I smile back before turning around to return to the warmth of the building. With too much on my mind to listen to his woes and unable to share the reason for my visit here, I'm unwilling to begin a conversation with a stranger.

Eventually I find a vending machine. Purchasing two coffees and a hot chocolate, I balance the three drinks on top of each other and make my way back towards the cubicle. I get half way, when I hear the unmistakable sound of Sam's voice up ahead.

"Two more minutes, please. Kate needs to know where we are." He is pleading with the nurse, who's pushing Jodie in a wheelchair.

I can't leave him for five minutes without drama. A simple text would suffice to let me know they have changed location. With the stack of drinks balanced precariously, I hasten my pace, smiling at Jodie, who appears entertained.

"Sam! Take this middle drink before I drop it please." I say to distract him. He's startled by my voice. "Jodie, I will carry yours as its very hot. You can have it just as soon as we arrive wherever it is we're heading."

"I've managed to find somewhere more comfortable." The nurse says, with pride. "We need to get there fast, otherwise someone else will. Your colleague here isn't making that easy for me."

"He's funny though!" Jodie says, laughing.

"You think so?" I say, shooting Sam a look. "You should try spending a whole day with him."

Jodie, now settled into her private room, thanks me for her hot chocolate. We're finally starting to build trust between the three of us by just spending time together. However, I was sure that once the police arrived she would start clamming up again and I didn't expect they would allow us to interview her.

A social worker had been called by the hospital. Being in the foster care system, Jodie already had one allocated to her and she had been reached. Given the extraordinary circumstances, she was willing to attend despite not being on call.

Various medical staff drifted in and out, made observations and punched the information into some kind of electronic touch-screen device – handwritten notes a thing of the past here. Sam excused himself and returned a little time later with a stack of activities he'd bought from the hospital shop for Jodie to enjoy.

His motivations weren't completely innocent. Amongst the items were a notebook and some felt tip pens. I knew what he wanted from her – but it was a long shot.

Drawn to the pens immediately, Jodie started to draw. It was crude, as you'd expect from a five-year old. Choosing the black pen, she drew a rough rectangular shape with stick arms and legs and a large circle head, without a neck. Changing to brown, she gave her image long brown hair and two eyes. Changing again, this time to red, she drew lips – giving the face a sad look. Still using the red pen, she then scribbled all over the image. Picking the black pen back up, she then drew a blob with a line sticking out from it at the end of one of the arms. I was expecting her to do the same the other side, thinking it was a hand. She didn't, and I realised it may be a gun, but it wasn't identifiable.

Having watched the process of the image come into shape,

as basic as it is, my excitement was becoming difficult to contain. Was it possible we were looking at the first image of the murderer? Was she trying to tell us that the person who entered her home, brandishing a gun was a woman rather than Ashbeck? Did the red scribbling represent blood? I had so many questions formulating for her but knew I couldn't ask. Without consulting a psychiatrist, I'm also fully aware I might be reading too much into the images a five-year-old might produce.

Turning the page, she tore the next clean sheet out. Still using the black pen, she drew an incomprehensible shape in the centre. Placing the pen down, she then holds her drawing up and rips it in half and places it on top of her first picture. She had seen the ace of spades, and the act of it being torn in half. This was vital evidence.

Jodie is an incredible little girl.

Sam and I exchanged glances, our eyes wide. We both knew that this little girl was capable of giving us what we need – she could identify the murderer if we could gain permission to get that information from her. That would be the most difficult part because of her being so young. Unfortunately, we'd have a hard time convincing her social worker that it would be of benefit. There would be protocol to follow, of course, before Sam would be allowed to ask Jodie to describe the person she watched kill the other girl in her room. It would be traumatising, but it could save other lives. This little girl was our only hope for justice for the rest of her family and the future survival of others. It was up to us to sell the notion that, somehow, it would benefit Jodie to do this for us.

I had no idea how Sam had learnt this skill – to sit and listen to someone describe a person they saw at a crime and for him to sketch a decent enough image for identification. It was an unusual talent, but one that has proven its worth so many times in his career.

"Sam, let me be the one to ask. I'm slightly more diplomatic than you." I smile.

"I don't rate our chances."

"Me either, but we need to ask."

"It would help so much."

"This already has."

"Yep."

When, eventually, the social worker made her entrance Jodie was pleased to see a familiar face. Before introductions were made the lady made a fuss of her.

Turning to Sam, she held out her hand and they shook,

"I'm Sadie Kemp. I work for the council and am Jodie's case worker. I found her placement with Mr and Mrs Collins. Jodie has been in my care for a while now. Thank you for taking good care of her."

"I'm Sam Cooper and," turning to me, he adds, "this is Katie-Ann Warwick, or Kate." Sadie turns to me and we shake hands. Pleasantries exchanged, Sam and I move to the side of the room to allow Sadie and Jodie time to talk. Sadie touches the pictures but does not comment. She turns her head towards us momentarily before her attention returns to the child.

"I just need to talk to Sam and Kate, okay. I won't be long, and we will be just outside the door. Could I please borrow your pictures?"

"No. They are for the police when they arrive. It's what I saw."

"Have you been asked to do these?"

"No."

"Okay."

"I'll only be a few minutes, okay."

"Okay. Will Sam and Kate be coming back too?"

"We won't go anywhere without saying goodbye," I assure her.

We exit, and she looks sad. My heart aches once again.

"This is not an ideal place to be speaking," I start. "However, you need to be aware that Jodie is a living witness that we believe has links to a case we are working on. The main perpetrator in that case is a very dangerous man and that places her at high risk. She has witnessed horrors tonight that may haunt her for the rest of her life. We cannot enter into the details of the case at this point, but the person we think is behind this attack likes that concept and he will play on the fact there is a survivor. We need him caught."

"The picture Jodie has drawn is very clearly a woman," Sadie interrupts.

"Yes, it appears so." Sam states.

"What is the significance of the other image? The one she has torn in half."

"That is crucial, but we are sorry to not be able to share why with you right now. You will be present at Jodie's interview so will learn about it then." He pauses, "or at least afterwards if she doesn't speak out."

Sadie nods at Sam, adding "She was doing so well. This will set her back. I had found her a permanent placement and that will fall through now. That makes my heart ache."

"Jodie is a material witness and due to the nature of our case will need to enter the witness protection programme. This will be a very scary time for her." I look at Sadie before adding "There is one thing I need to ask you, and it is vital to our investigation."

"Go on, you can ask."

"Because of the evidence found at the scene we were expecting a male perpetrator, but as you've seen, Jodie's image suggests otherwise." I pause to allow this to sink in, "Sam has this talent and a fantastic track record at solving crimes using it. Would you permit Jodie, as her appropriate adult, to describe the woman to him and have him sketch her? If we could have an image of her and put that through our database, we might well have her on record already and that would give us a head start on catching her and removing her from the street."

"That is a tall ask of a five-year old."

"We know that," Sam says, but Kate and I won that little girl over today. We've not probed or asked questions. We have literally sat with her, provided her with hot chocolate and company. We've turned a shocked, silent little girl into someone who has started to open up. She'll have to talk at some point, it may as well be to me."

Nodding, Sadie turns and opens the door to return to Jodie.

It wasn't a 'no'. Promising.

We followed her, and within five minutes two police officers turned up. Expecting her to be shy and crumble I feel a nervousness come over me. Instead, she comes to life. Sam returns to his seat at Jodie's request and she reaches for his hand. I remain near the door and Sadie takes the other seat beside the bed.

After introductions and relevance to our presence and everyone showing their identification badges, Jodie begins to reveal what she has heard in fine detail, beyond her young years. She explains how she hid behind the panelled wall because she was afraid of her foster father. He'd hit her a couple of times if she didn't sleep. Learning that her older sister was the girl that she'd shared a bedroom with and that she'd watched a woman walk into their room through the crack in the wooden panel and heard the gun go off sent shivers down my spine. Without emotion, she shares that she'd been too scared to move. Reaching to pick up her pictures she hands them to Sam, who passes them over to the officer closest to him.

"The woman took something from her pocket and had ripped it in half before putting it on my sister," she said. After some thought, added "one of the black cards we play snap with."

Sadie Kemp made eye contact with me.

Jodie's story continued, as she explained what she had heard. The woman moved onto the next bedroom. We had a sequence of events for the deaths on that floor of the house. The male police officer took notes, while the female asked questions. Sam jumped at his chance when she asked if she could describe the woman that Jodie saw come into the bedroom. He took out his notebook and a pen. As this brave little girl begins her description, he etches marks onto paper. Both officers stopped and enquired.

"Just drawing what I hear. I will show you when I'm done."

Giving him a blank look, they continue writing down their description as Jodie speaks.

With the colour slowly draining from Sam's face, I walk over and glance over his shoulder. A familiar face stares up at me from the page in his hand. Sam looks up at me and our eyes meet. Having listened to the description I'm now drawn back to every detail and am making comparisons: each of them is clear to me. Sam does not get this process wrong. If he's right this time however, our investigation is compromised.

Someone in the room speaks, I'm not sure who.

"You two look like you've just seen a ghost."

8

REFLECTION

Carl Ashbeck entered my life just over four years ago during a troubling case that resulted in his arrest for kidnap and murder. Customs and Excise were running a case alongside ours for people trafficking, he'd been charged separately for that too.

I'd been lucky, I guess. Despite three attempts on my life, I'd refused to play his game. I hope he never makes a captor of me – a thought I refuse to comprehend. His victims didn't always survive. I'd viewed their bodies on gurneys in morgues and on photographs. The images were etched into my mind as if I'd seen them an hour ago.

Others had survived their ordeals and were living with the physical and psychological scars. I'd never fathomed how they'd managed any level of normality and until last autumn I'd had no choice but allow them to disappear into the witness protection programme. After Ashbeck escaped from prison, I came into contact with two of his surviving victims. Humbled by their resilience and determination to succeed in life, they were living proof of how diverse we can be if our focus is on being positive to overcome adversity. I'd learnt so much from meeting these women; in a way they'd given me a degree of closure. When I looked at the mutilation Ashbeck has caused on the skin of one I no longer saw her wounds – instead my mind was transported to the artwork she'd had tattooed to disguise them. Having met her through her husband (a police officer in Great Yarmouth) last year, she'd taken me to one side in her home, privately, and shown me the majority of the artwork. A privilege that she'd do that, after all she'd been through.

"You've viewed my body so many times, Kate," she'd said. "Once more makes no difference to me. I think it will be good for you to see how I've altered the scars and I need you to see me for who I am now," she continued to chat with ease as she slipped her dress off her shoulders and allowed it to fall to the floor.

Jane Gosling was covered in the prettiest tattoos: flowers, butterflies, birds and fairies that were very cleverly placed to disguise her scars. They were very effective, and I had found it hard to turn my eyes away from her body – she allowed me time to absorb her artwork and her beauty. When she'd had enough, she dipped down to the floor and gathered her dress. At this point I turned away and gave her privacy while she covered herself. Once she was dressed, a silence fell between us and we gave each other a long hug. This moment that we'd shared had certainly helped me overcome the fear I'd held that Ashbeck's survivors couldn't possibly have made a decent life for themselves. This brave, courageous woman had shown perseverance, determination and inner strength that gave me hope for Mel.

Mandy Wiseman had shown her bravery in a different way. She was bold and the centre of attention within her community and faced her fears head on. When it became apparent that

Ashbeck was a threat to her once again, she refused to move away. She'd rather stay and face whatever he had planned, rather than spend the rest of her life running from him. Unsure how she was feeling, I'd asked her why she wouldn't move, and she simply stated that she no longer allowed anyone to control how she reacted. That Ashbeck would not get inside her head again. If he, or a member of his gang turned up on her doorstep then she would win, or they would, and she accepted those consequences.

Meeting both women had been eye-opening for me and they'd wanted to remain in contact. No longer a police officer, they had begged me to keep in touch and I'd done just that. Staying in touch with my old friends Jen Jennings and Mel Sage is also important to me. Not a week goes by when I don't phone all four women. Mel, Jen and I go back years, and I try to get us all chatting together as often as possible. Both women need the support for very different reasons but both of them because of Ashbeck. We are bonded in a way that other people could never understand.

Ashbeck's timing was impeccable. The very day Sam and I began a personal relationship, he escaped from prison. Hardly the start we'd needed. I'd had a choice but couldn't resist joining Sam in an undercover mission. Mel was missing and the evidence was pointing towards kidnap – we believed, rightly so, this was on Ashbeck's orders.

Sam and I had been pushed to our limits during this operation.

Our working relationship remains intact as does our friendship – just – but our intimate relationship is non-existent right now. Unable to cope with the loss of Sam's son, Charlie, both of us were drifting from one day to the next with all desire vanished from us.

As our mission came to an end we forged new alliance with Kerry Preston who heads the private investigation company we now work for. Answering directly to the home office she's a powerful woman with a computer system that astounds me. Kerry's clearance on highly sensitive data, is outstanding. The trust they put in her obviously reflective of the work she must have done for them when she worked on past cases.

During our undercover operation we'd discovered many things. It became apparent we only trust each other. I can categorically say there is nobody else in this world I trust more than Sam. We'd already placed each other's life in the other's hands years before – we know we can rely on each other. There is only one other person that comes close, and that is our friend JJ. So far he has remained loyal to us.

Trust is everything in this world. Whenever we discovered something new in this case it was through someone having let us down. Someone we thought we could trust. It comes to the point when trust vanishes and all concept of respect for the force in which you were once so proud is put in the balance. Corruption spreading from the very top and seeping through the hierarchy kept us from capturing Ashbeck and has caused much turmoil. The people involved won't survive, of that I'm sure. Paranoia now plays a huge role in my life. Perhaps I'm overly guarded but cases like this get to you eventually.

Establishing a new team working against Ashbeck had pooled new knowledge and that had proven vital. We know so much more about him now. Some was fact and some circumstantial – but that's a good place to start. While searching for information Sam and I discovered a link between Ashbeck's businesses and interests; the logos he used were all linked through symbolism. We were led to a website giving details of the illuminati. This was a man who had become obsessed. The deeper we looked into his world the more we discovered: somehow, he had learnt their knowledge and way of thinking. This placed him in a strong position, in his own mind, which is never a good prospect when you're dealing with a psychopath.

Sam also believed that Ashbeck may have links to the American military: to Vietnam in particular. Already familiar with the brutality of his acts, when Sam learnt that the ace of spades playing card was his signature he was able to make this association. During the original investigation I'd requested the involvement of Interpol which had been refused by my boss. This had now been approved and we are waiting results – I am meeting with the gov in a couple of days to find out if anything has developed from it – he just doesn't know it yet. Making a mental note to contact him, I continue with my day.

9

OLD TIMER

Having moved into a three-story property along an unmade lane that runs parallel to the River Blackwater in Maldon, Ashbeck was living a quiet life. Far from the bustling city he'd been used to before prison, this place was giving him some space. He needed time to reflect and to plan his next move.

The remoteness was comforting and the closeness to the water was helping to keep his mind calm. It was the one thing he'd truly craved from inside his prison cell. There wasn't anything that he missed about prison. Prison had changed a lot about him and the need for being alone was one of those things. Needing to be the centre of attention was no longer his priority, he'd taken a step back from his business. That side of his life was ticking along nicely without him and he'd grown used to not being involved while inside. He was an old man now and recognised it was time to take a step back, to pass his legacy onto someone else. He'd made his choice.

One regret he'd had was getting the eye tattoos on his forehead. It had been such a statement of defiance at the time, but now they hindered his ability to blend into society.

Having such identifiable marks on his face could so easily be his downfall. Every time he ventured out he'd wear a bandanna over his head, making sure to secure it tightly, covering the ink – it was the only way.

He wasn't alone. There were a couple of other people wearing bandannass in the town, especially near the Hythe. Ashbeck spent most of his outside time hanging about there: watching the boats, the people and mesmerised by the movement of the water. He hadn't expected to see old-fashioned Thames Barges still working outside the city, it made him feel at home. Now used for tourist trips on the river, weddings and all manner of civilised events, these magnificent vessels were once cargo ships: their enormous red ochre sails iconic to this area.

Despite his age, the urges were building again. His mind festered new ideas when all he truly desired was peace. He'd hoped that prison would have yielded change in him rather than intensify what he required. Something had shifted. His thoughts and needs had evolved in a way that scared him. Having given permission to three members of his gang to murder on his behalf, he knew bodies would begin to appear in various locations and confuse the authorities. This allows him to develop his next move – his personal journey that would transform his hell into something spectacular.

Selecting his next victim has been easy. The strawberry blonde woman from next door. Watching her from the comfort of his own home an added bonus, giving him unlimited access without raising any alarm or suspicion. She was a creature of habit; he knew he'd chosen well. Not only was she beautiful – it would please him to be in her company – but she'd prove easy prey. Managing to avoid any form of contact so far he was enjoying this young woman very much.

She'd woken the monster within him. Aroused his need to kill and he'd planned with precise detail his next move. A moment of truth. Of glorious re-birth: like a phoenix rising from the ashes. Timing will be fundamental, and he needed Shadow to be close. He was waiting for her call.

Placing his trust in a woman had surprised him. Yet since the death of his sergeant all those years ago in Vietnam she was the only other person that had understood him. Not once had she shown fear in his company. Respect, yes, but never fear. He appreciated her confidence around him.

She'd suffered all her life, like he had. Convinced this connected them, he'd allowed them to bond. Loving her in a fatherly way he'd trained her for this moment.

Kneeling at his altar, he prayed to his new God that it would be time to act soon. He longed to act. To feel the stickiness of her blood and watch the life drain from her eyes, savouring the moment and remembering the others. Dreaming of what he might plan for Katie-Ann Warwick would be just that – a dream. For that pleasure now passed to someone else. His agenda had changed.

He dreamt of enlightenment.

10

RELOCATION

Jodie had spent the night at a safe house, her location unknown even to us. Wondering how safe she really was, my mind kept drifting to Ashbeck's original victims who'd been part of the witness protection programme who had been relocated under the watchful eyes of members of his gang. We'd yet to establish how this occurred – to think that Jodie could be facing the same fate, beyond any rational processing I'm willing to comprehend this morning – the thought we could be placing this little girl in jeopardy enough to boil the blood in my veins.

Alarms that sounded at four in the morning weren't normally welcome but today's couldn't be avoided. Having had a shower and thrown on comfortable but smart clothes I'd headed out the door and hoped that Sam would be outside his building with two coffees in his hands.

Running slightly late, I'm relieved that Sam is sitting on the wall waiting for me when I arrive. He seems energetic as he springs to his feet and I have to lean over to open the passenger door as he is laden with drinks and food. Showing my appreciation with a smile on my face as way of greeting, he climbs in and I take what I can from him and locate it around the car.

We are part of something important today. Jodie goes deep into hiding. Relocated for her protection and we were part of the relay team that would provide the transport for that. As far as I know we were the second leg of the journey. Meeting at a pre-arranged location I'd yet to learn the registration number of the vehicle she would arrive in. All in good time. Her chaperone would pass me a sealed envelope with a postcode that I would enter into my GPS for directions. She or he would then watch me delete this information at the end of the journey.

"You don't call me pumpkin anymore," he says, referring to the nickname I used while we were undercover last year.

"No," I laughed, "it's been a while. You know I only called you that to annoy Phil?"

"I know. Kinda grew to like it though."

"Hmmm."

"What do you mean, hmmm?"

"Sam, when we went undercover our situation wasn't ideal. We knew we risked losing what we started. You know, us. I'm not saying we're done, but we're definitely struggling. This case is eating me up from the inside. I really believe we need to be Sam and Kate again." Pausing, I glance at him before continuing. "I know some things can't be the same but it's where we started."

"We were so traumatised from the accident and losing Charlie," he says "that we didn't stop being James and Lori when we came home. Kate we've been acting as if we're still undercover. You know we never had a debrief. Jade should have called us in. Instead she sent our papers with someone else. She should have insisted."

"So, from today we start over," I am asking, "as Sam and Kate to try and get us back?" Sudden calmness settles over me and Sam relaxes into his seat.

"Sounds perfect to me."

11

DANCING STARS

Laughter fills the air as our new acquaintances share stories of one another with us in their local pub. Their past antics have Sam and I doubled over. In unison they turn to us, the city cops turned private investigators. The room becomes silent as they wait for a story, or two. Sam looks at me and begins to unbutton his shirt.

"Sam, no." I quietly say.

"Kate is my hero," he states, with conviction. As he slides his shirt down his back he turns to show his scar. "She pressed her hands into this knife wound until the ambulance arrived, she saved my life." He leaned over and planted a kiss on my cheek to an uproar of cheers.

"Your turn Princess, what have I done for you?"

"I am not showing you guys what Sam has done for me!" I say, pointing my finger at each of them in turn. "He has saved my life too. I have a similar wound."

"I've seen it!" JJ steps in. "Kate's wound is worse than Sam's. She was lucky to survive."

"Oh, come on. Now you have to show us!" Frank insists.

"I certainly do not!" As important as it is we bond with the team, they will not see my scar.

Chatting continues as we get to know each other, laughter erupting often. Frank and Sam find a quiet spot to have a private talk. Leaving them to it, I figure it's about time Sam stands on his own feet where talking about Charlie is concerned. Curiosity pricks at me as to how far into his private life Sam had allowed Frank, knowing that not many met his family. Leaning towards JJ, I quietly ask.

"They worked well together but he never met the family like us and Phil."

"No one else?"

"You got it."

Its startling how intoxicated Sam is considering he'd only had two pints in an hour. Concerned, I suggest he sleeps while I drive but he's having none of it – instead he talks freely, the alcohol in his system loosening his reserve for the first time in ages. Learning about the difficult time he's been having since Charlie's death wasn't surprising but hard non-the-less. Guilt burns deep within me because I've distanced myself but the wedge that we've developed is a two-way thing. Despite us still working together and seeing each other most days our intimacy has become non-existent, and I didn't know how to fix it.

Reaching over and placing a hand on his thigh, I give it a squeeze.

"I miss you so much," he says.

"Me too, Sam. Me too."

"Stay tonight, for dinner at least?"

Glancing over, I smile.

"Only dinner?"

Smiling back at me he runs his finger-tips over the top of my hand and up my arm as far as he can, restricted by my jacket. Goosebumps form as tingles shoot along my arm.

"It will be so good to hold you in my arms, to warm your cold body against me."

"This case is pushing us to our boundaries."

"It's already pushed me to mine, Princess."

I know, I understand that."

"Curry?"

"Sounds good."

Sam dials and orders. He doesn't need to ask what I want to eat, he knows. Just as I don't need to know where to drive to collect our food. A contentment settles over me as we make small talk for the rest of the journey home.

Sitting with foil containers between us, Sam and I share our food and can't stop making eyes at each other. Our legs touch under the table.

"Let's make a promise," he says. "Tonight, is about us, and only us." His way of saying work is off limits.

"Deal."

Raising my glass of water, I clink it with his can of lager. Enjoying conversation like we used to, we begin relaxing. A refreshing change from the bickering pair we'd become in recent months. I'm not naive – we need more than one evening to repair the damage in order to resolve our issues – but tonight we'd made a great start. Togetherness was something we both needed right now.

Having agreed to stay the night, I needed to pop home to collect a few bits – we didn't want to stay at mine as the pull of work would be too much having all our files there. We made a pact. I'd make a dash for what I needed while Sam cleared away our mess and poured some wine.

Perfect.

Despite me only living two streets away I take my car. I'm not in the mood to walk and neither of us think it's safe to do so this late at night. Both Sam and I have allocated parking, so it's easy. Making a dash towards the lift, I only take a few paces before noticing a familiar face. Someone from earlier in the day, perhaps. Maybe someone from the team, even, I couldn't be sure. Uneasiness spread through me and the hairs on my arms stood to attention.

Since my stabbing men in hoodies put me on edge and he is wearing one. Ashbeck's gang also wear them. This man emerged from behind a pillar and was now approaching fast. A deep furrow evident between his eyes, his clenched jaw showing a determination I didn't like the look of. Within a moment my handbag was over my head, satchel style so both hands were free and in front of me, ready to defend. Knowing I was in trouble, with no time to turn back. I was on high alert. Anxiety has hold as his body impacts against mine. My legs, weak from my frightened state, didn't put up any resistance as his full weight hit me and we tumbled towards concrete. Fast to straddle me as my shoulders and head crash against the floor, he pins me to the ground. I focus on his face, my vision blurring. Swinging my right arm outwards, I take aim with determination to fight back.

His right fist meets the left side of my head first, ensuring dizziness and disorientation. I watch as tiny stars dance before my eyes, the fight in me escaping with every breath. Struggling to keep my eyes open and my mind on the situation, I feel myself drift upwards – a lightness escaping from my body and a sudden view of myself from above. Unsure what is happening to me I watch myself as he rips my blouse open. Trying to scream for the body that lays beneath me, frozen to the spot but no words escape. How can this be happening? There must be something I can do. How can I be watching myself like this?

Again, unsure of why or how, I'm suddenly at one as reality returns and my mind returns to my body. Now looking back up at the man on top of me, the mean look within his eyes draws my attention to him. Focussing on his features, through my blurry vision I lay in fear as he reaches inside his jacket pocket and removes something. Convinced he's about to hold a knife to my throat and that I will die this time my muscles begin shaking involuntary.

"Back off, bitch," he scolds as he places something inside my bra before he stands and disappears into the shadows.

Trembling, I gradually ease myself into the sitting position, raise my knees and rest my head, allowing the new wave of stars to pass.

Gradually, as my bearings are regained, I stand. There is no way I can drive. My vision is blurred to the point I can only see shapes. Making my way towards the street I stagger from the shelter of the covered car park, my hands keeping my blouse firmly closed. Sam's flat is only two streets away – close enough but I'm not sure if I can walk that far. Knowing I must try, my steps are unsteady as the approach to Sam's building takes forever. Usually a walk of five minutes, I'm convinced twenty have passed, with many passers-by unyielding with their help. The rudeness of people never failing to astound me.

Finally, as I near the front door of his apartment block a woman I recognise holds the door and waits for me. Knowing she's one of Sam's neighbours, but not her name I finally have someone to rely on. Realising I'm in some sort of trouble she takes my arm and helps me. Wondering what I must look like, we link arms and take the lift to the fourth floor. Leaning against her for support as shock settles over me I allow her to take control. Unable to talk she guides me to Sam's front door – her fist pounds upon it until he answers.

"Louise, Hi," he says, casually and then spots me. "Oh fuck! What the hell happened to you, Princess?"

"I found her like this outside the front door."

I stumble over the threshold, and he attempts to support me. Holding my hands, palms up, he realises he needs to back off. He cannot touch me.

"Louise, have you touched Kate?"

"Yes, I helped her. Why?"

"You need to come in. Sorry."

Standing in the middle of the kitchen I can feel my body trembling. Knowing what was needed I stand still and wait for Sam to join me. When he does, Louise is following with a concerned look on her face. Having helped me out, she's involved herself in our case – and is very obviously unhappy about it.

"All I need from you is a swab to rule out your DNA. You've touched Kate's clothes. It won't hurt, and it won't take long."

"Okay," Louise is compliant. "Whatever you need."

Sam swabs the inside of her mouth, places it into an evidence bag and fills out the label.

"What about Kate. Won't you need her clothes? Kate would you like me to stay?"

I shake my head, still unable to talk. I need her gone.

"We will be fine, thanks. We know what to do. Kate can trust me."

"If you're sure, sweetie?"

I nod my head.

Sam walks Louise to the door and returns to me. I am not ready to let go of my shirt and I stand there my arms wrapped tightly around my body.

"Kate, you've been here for me through some very dark times, it's my turn. I'm not blessed with half the patience you've shown me and I'm fully aware of how ungracefully I've behaved recently. Yet you trusted me enough to come bashing on my door tonight so please trust me with what's gone on since I saw you an hour ago."

He is, of course, completely right. I don't trust anyone else the way I trust Sam.

Tears form. I make no effort in controlling them as they freefall down my cheeks. Reaching inside my pocket I pull out latex gloves and ask Sam to wear them. He has evidence to collect.

"No, I will wear my own gloves. Yours might be compromised." He removes gloves from his kit and places them on his hands. Gently, he takes my hands in his and unfolds my arms from my body because I've wrapped them around my body again. Starting the slow process of removing fibres and evidencing them before removing my clothing, one item at a time, again each item is bagged and labelled as he goes. When my top is removed Sam notices something sticking out of the top of my bra.

He looks at me and from the look in my eyes he knows I don't need telling what it is – an ace of spades playing card.

Ashbeck's signature.

I don't need swabs taken from my mouth, but we do them anyway. Sam also takes swabs from my chest.

Standing in Sam's kitchen in just my knickers, feeling emotionally and physically drained, a feeling of agitation washes over me. This evening was supposed to be about us. Not about my vulnerability. Yet here I stand having been processed for a crime by the man who wants to take me to bed. My body aches from impact and my head pounds from concussion. I'm not sure how much longer I can stand here, exposed.

"All done. Let's get you to the shower. You go through and I'll be along with a clean towel." Privacy not on Sam's agenda, because that's not how we work. It's never how it's been between us.

Uncomfortable parading about naked, tonight was certainly no different – wrapping my arms around my body for protection that made no difference, I make my way towards Sam's bedroom. The sight of the bed we once shared stirring emotions within me. Averting my eyes, I enter the bathroom and turn on the shower, while it warms I slip out of my knickers.

Water stings the grazes on my shoulders and back, but the need to feel clean overpowers the pain. I allow the jets to massage my sore muscles before stepping back and soaking my hair. Blood streaks down my body and pools around my feet. Not realising my head was cut I run my fingers through my hair to explore the site. Tender and swollen but grazed rather than cut. Squeezing shampoo into my hand, I brace myself as I massage it into my hair. The stinging sensation of the soap is incredible, bringing tears to my eyes as suds mingle with blood and run down my face. Allowing tears to freefall, I'm unaware of being watched.

Turning around, I allow the water to pound against my face, as the sobbing commences. It's relentless. Hitting the power, the water ceases. Red eyed I step out and Sam is waiting for me with a towel and he wraps me in it; gathering me in his arms and pulling me in close. Unable to stop the tears, they continue – for Charlie, for us and for my attack.

"I've found you some clothes for tonight. They're on the bed. Then we need to talk." Standing, he holds out his hand. I place mine into it, and he leads me into the bedroom. "I'll be in the kitchen when you're ready."

Describing my attack and my attacker, Sam listens, studies me and makes marks on a notebook. Knowing he'll be sketching the face as I describe it, my eyes are closed as I reach deep inside of me for the details.

"Ready to see it?" He asks when we're done.

I nod, and when he turns the notebook to face me I'm startled with his artwork one more time.

"Make the jaw-line more rigid. Squarer, somehow. Then you'll have him captured," I think for a moment before adding "like he's gritting his teeth."

After a few more lines, he shows me again and its spot on. I nod, and he takes an image with his mobile and sends it to our new colleagues. He also sends it to his old ones at Paddington station and calls in a favour.

Both of us have been anticipating Ashbeck to make his presence known. Now he had I need a drink. Not normally one to turn to alcohol under such situations, Sam watches me as I raid his whisky. Selecting the first I find, having no idea when it comes to such matters, I open the bottle and inhale the fumes, sneering.

"If you are going to drink my best malt, you can at least be polite about it, that stuff isn't cheap," he says with a wink.

I take two glasses from the cupboard and take everything into the lounge – my way of saying that I'm done with talking for the night.

Collapsing into the soft leather I'm suddenly exhausted. Sam doesn't follow immediately. By the time he appears, bowl of water in one hand and cotton lint in the other I'm already on my second drink. It burns on its way down and I'm feeling the effects.

"Can I sleep on your sofa?"

"On my sofa?" He asks, with a disappointed look across his face. "No, Kate. You can sleep in my bed. Kick me out if you need to but I'm not letting you have the sofa."

Disappearing off he doesn't leave me to my thoughts for long. Returning, he places a towel on the arm of the sofa and the bowl onto it. Kneeling in front of me, he straddles one of my legs, his knees buried into the sofa cushions, and starts cleaning my wounds. I'm not making it easy, remaining slouched deeply in the seat, large whisky in hand. Supporting himself by placing his left hand on the headrest, working on my face with his right, each time he replaces the lint his face is just that little bit closer to mine. Unsure if it's the water or blood I can feel trickling down my face, I swipe it with the back of my hand. He gently stops me. I'm edgy and fully aware of it.

Placing my hand on his right shoulder I gradually work my way around to the back of his neck. My thumb gently caressing his skin, my fingers lost in his hair. My body is awakening. He continues to cleanse my wounds when all I want is for him to kiss me, hold me and to remove my clothes.

Finally finished, he peels himself away from me and vanishes with everything he's used while I sit and sip at whisky. Despite the warm glow in my throat and stomach, coldness begins to overcome my body and I begin to shiver. I'm close to tears again and force them back, biting my lip.

Returning, Sam sits beside me and takes me in his arms. Collapsing into him I allow an outflow of emotion as my relentless sobbing returns. Neither of us talk as I allow what I've been holding inside for months to escape. After the tears and body heaves stop he continues to hold me for a long time. Having found a loose thread on his shirt I'm fiddling with it, somewhat preoccupied.

"I'm going to take a shower and then we are going to the hospital. I'd feel better if you were checked out."

"I'm fine. Yes, it hurts but it's going to. Crying hasn't helped with that. The stars have gone, and my vision is normal."

"I'm not convinced, and I can't help but worry about you."

Smiling I stand and walk towards the bedroom, with Sam following. Allowing the dressing gown to fall to the floor, he watches as I remove the t-shirt and boxers I've borrowed and walk into the bathroom. Turning on the shower, I wait until the water is hot. Within a moment Sam is naked and his hands are encasing my waist. We step forward under the water. The cubical door closes as I turn to face him, sliding my hands up his firm chest. Our lips meet, and pain shoots up the left side of my face. I wince – not wanting the moment spoilt, I slide my arms around his wet body and pull him into a close embrace. Water cascades over and around us and stings my bruised skin. Sam reaches for the shower gel and he washes hastily, never taking his gaze from me. Hitting the water for it to stop he exits and grabs the towels, wrapping me up first then himself.

Taking my hand, he leads me into his bedroom and around the other side of the bed. Turning me to towards his full-length mirror, he forces me to look. I'd not seen my wounds yet.

"Take a good look, Katie-Ann Warwick and you tell me if you wouldn't want to take me to the hospital if this was role reversal."

He has never, once called me by my full name.

Swallowing hard, I look up and begin to take in my reflection. I turn slightly to look at my back and allow the towel to drop away from me. Bruising and grazes adorn my body – I'm going to be sore tomorrow. What startles me the most is the state of my face. My left cheek and eye are both swollen and bruised. I'm also supporting a cut above my eye that is gaping and weeping slightly.

"At the very least, I'd like you to have stitches above your eye, I don't have any wound strips."

"I have some in my bag."

Rolling his eyes Sam goes in search of my handbag. When he returns, he empties the contents on the bed – all manner of items tumbling onto the duvet.

"In the zipped part" I say. It never sits well with him when he's rifling through my bag and I'm trying not to smile at the look on his face. It hurts too much to smile.

Eventually he finds what he's searching for and I sit on the end of the bed. He takes his time fixing my face while I make the most of his almost naked body. My hands find their way to the back of his legs and gradually work their way upward under the tiny towel he has wrapped around his waist. Lingering on his naked buttocks my fingers dance over his skin before I pull him closer to me.

"Hey, let me finish this first," he says playfully.

Gradually moving my hands further towards the front of his body, his smile widens as I tease my fingers over him. When, finally he's done, the contents of my bag are hastily shoved back before he leaps onto the bed and under the covers. Joining him, he scoops me up in his arms. Every cell in my body awakens to his touch as his fingers dance across my naked skin: they leave a trail of fire in their wake.

Rolling over so I face him, with our legs entwined, and our bodies responding to each other for the first time in a very long time. One hand works its way under his neck, pulling him in closer. Finger nails on my free hand gently tickle delicate places I know will drive him crazy. Within a heartbeat our lips connect sending surges of energy through me and causing sharp pain to my bruised face. Sam's touch is so gentle, so caring, so loving. I ache for him. But I ache for our closeness more.

I've missed that.

It lasts just a moment – fatigue sets in as the day takes its toll, my eyes roll to the back of my head. Unable to fight my sudden tiredness I feel myself drift into sleep.

12

TURNED OVER

Sam emerges from under the duvet first, unaware that he's disturbed me. Having reached under his pillow he now walks towards his wardrobe. I watch through slitted eyelids as he hides a handgun inside his safe and locks the door.

Remaining motionless, lost for words and deep in thought I watch as he walks out the room. Having always told me he hates guns, that they have no place in civilian life, he has me scared. When I can find the words, I'll hold him to a conversation about this. But not now.

I've woken with pain in my head and it throbs – extending across my forehead into my temples and down into my face. Lifting my head from my pillows fills me with dread and I brace myself. Rolling onto my side, I slowly ease myself onto my elbows and see how I feel. Pain shoots through my back and shoulders. Fighting back tears, my eyes begin to sting.

Today was going to be one of those tough ones and I want to remain under the duvet for its entirety. The first surge of pain passed and so I move a little more until I'm sitting on the side of the bed – the room spinning out of control. Nausea consumes me and its all I can do to stop myself from succumbing to its affects. Unsure if I'm suffering the effects of concussion or whisky I allow my head to settle. The smell of coffee and bacon drifts in the air, encouraging me to move.

After visiting the bathroom, I grab Sam's dressing gown and painkillers from my bag before making my way towards the kitchen. Walking up to Sam, I kiss him on the lips.

"Not a word, I'm fine."

"Have you even looked this morning?"

"Not yet."

"Hmmm."

My whisky glass from last night had been washed and was draining on the side. Filling it from the tap, I wash down the pills.

"What were they?"

"Paracetamol and ibuprofen. Nothing major."

"Pain level?"

"About to reduce."

"Not funny."

"Not laughing."

Sam was cooking eggs, bacon and mushrooms but the way I liked them. Having already grilled the bacon and fried the mushrooms in butter he was now making a French omelette. Soft, creamy and well-seasoned he adds the mushrooms just before turning it onto a large oval platter. Criss-crossing the bacon over the top he places the plate in the middle of the table for us to share.

Topping our coffee mugs up from his percolator, I carry them to the table, sit and we eat.

I slip into the shower and allow the hot water to soothe my battered body. Within thirty seconds the cubical door opens, and Sam steps inside, wrapping me into his arms.

Spending just a short time enjoying the water and steam we allow our hands to wander and our bodies to press against each other. Responding to the tenderness of his touch, the way he looks at me and the way he makes me feel, I move my hands up his body, over his chest and reach for his shoulders and neck. Lifting myself up, never breaking eye contact as he slides his hands down my back towards my thighs. Wrapping my legs around his body as he guides me, we gently make love under jets of water.

Now running late on a morning that's far from normal we make a dash towards my place as I still need a change of clothes. Sam had reported my attack last night, forensics were processing the scene. The evidence we'd collected was in the boot of his car ready for us to drop at the station later today.

As we walk towards my flat the hairs on my arms stand to attention, and a shiver runs down my spine. Sam notices the shift in my mood.

"What have you picked up on?"

"I'm not sure."

As we turn the corner at the end of the hallway, it becomes obvious. My front door is ajar, and I hope we don't have another crime scene on our hands. Somehow, I know better.

My heart-rate soars as we approach. Sam, with a sudden

burst of energy, runs while my legs turn to jelly. They refuse to move any faster than a sluggish walk – carrying me almost motionlessly towards the inevitable. By the time I arrive, Sam's already inside with his gloves on and his mobile to his ear. I stand, my chin dropped as an automatic response. The devastation within my home, catastrophic. My living area is ransacked, and Sam is already on the phone requesting forensics. He is fuming.

"Someone we can trust. We need to leave them to it today. They will need to lock up."

"Sam, our files!" I look at him with horror in my eyes as we both dash towards the makeshift incident room. Expecting to see the door splintered, swinging on broken hinges. Relief it remained undamaged takes time to register. Handing the keys to Sam, he unlocks the door, still wearing gloves. We enter. Nothing has been disturbed and it takes us both a few more moments for this to register – having the contents of this room discovered would blow the case apart.

Through force of habit, neither of us touch anything: this room is treated as if it's a crime scene. We leave and re-lock the door. Forensics will have to wait if they want to view in here. No one will enter without Sam or me. Sensitive data adorns the walls, and all flat surfaces, including the floor. It cannot be photographed or removed as evidence.

Moving along to my bedroom, again Sam enters first. Nothing has been touched. Quickly grabbing fresh clothes, I change and place what I was wearing into the laundry before we return to the main living space where upturned furniture greets us once more. Nothing appears missing from what I can tell: scare tactics.

Phoning Kerry, I explain the situation and she promises she'd have someone with us within fifteen minutes because Sam and I have somewhere we needed to be.

This morning's briefing was the last place I wanted to be, but it was something I needed to do. Not only did I want to hear any laboratory results for myself I wanted to know if Jodie had spoken any more overnight. Information like this wasn't something I was willing to receive second hand.

Settling into the passenger seat, it made a change for Sam to be driving me around. Reaching for my seat belt, I cringe with pain hoping he's not noticed and determined to make it through the day without further mention of hospital. The painkillers have eased my headache a little: I'm taking that as a good sign.

Our meeting this morning is in Chelmsford, at police headquarters. They were dealing with the Collins's murders and were setting the wheels in motion for the protection of Jodie. Despite us not being able to reach her, one person was nominated to have contact with their team should news arise. Protocol needed to be followed in order that our witness remained protected at all times – that was definitely my main concern right now.

"Sam, we need to talk about your gun." I was out with it. Turning towards me, with shock on his face he responds in a whisper,

"You weren't supposed to see that!"

"Obviously," I say with sarcasm, "but I did, and that's not

the point."

Silence fell between us. Knowing he'd not be able to stand it for long, I allow it to consume us watching the uneasiness spreading over him.

"Since that night I've had this sense that he's coming for me. For us. The nights are particularly bad." Pausing and taking a deep sigh, he looks at me again to gauge my mood. "I don't sleep much. When I do, I get these nightmares and wake up in cold sweats, unable to breathe. The slightest sound from outside and I'm on high alert. So, there we go. Now you know." Again, he pauses but he's not finished. "It keeps me safe."

"No, Sam. It doesn't!" I study his face: looking ahead at the road, tears rolling down his cheeks it's as much as I can do to remain composed.

"I have no idea where you got it, but you do need to get rid of it. Sam, look at me." Pausing, I wait for him to face me. He doesn't.

"Sam!" I'm firmer, and he slowly turns around. Holding out my hand he removes his from the steering wheel and places it in mine. I give it a gentle squeeze before I continue. "Right. No more pushing me away. We got into this together, we work through it together. Sam, I can't even begin to imagine..."

"Please don't, not now," he interrupts me. "I don't want you to imagine that. You were there, you lost him too."

Removing my hand from his, I reach up and wipe a tear from his cheek, unsure how I've not cried but knowing Sam needs me to be strong.

"We get through today. Tonight, we sleep without the gun. Tomorrow it goes." I'm firm. I've just told him, in my own way, that I'm moving in. I've not asked, not given it any thought – it's just happening.

I hope I don't regret it.

Reaching towards me he kisses me full on the lips. "It's a deal. Have you just moved in?"

"I think I have," I say smiling. "Please watch the road."

Without doubt I was angry with Sam for having the gun. He wasn't licensed and who knew what crime it may be linked to. How he'd even managed to get hold of it baffled me right now – I knew my curiosity would get the better of me! Now wasn't the time to ask. It saddened me he'd not shared how deeply he'd been suffering but more so that I hadn't spotted the signs myself. I'd not noticed him awake last night, but I'd not been on top form.

As much as I understand Sam's insecurity and anxiety because of my own, I'm struggling to get past his need for the gun other than because of his military past. We've never talked about his experiences of war and right now I'm contemplating the combined effect this and losing Charlie have had – is Sam experiencing flashbacks as part of post-traumatic stress disorder?

Making a pact with myself to help him through this difficult patch I try to push these issues to the back of my mind for now. The day ahead presents its own challenges and we need to refocus before reaching our meeting. A change of subject is needed.

"How are we going to explain the state you're in?" He asks.

"Tell the truth."

"Every detail?"

"Every detail," I look at him, "they need to know what they're dealing with. We have a woman who appears to be murdering on Ashbeck's orders and he's now sending gang members to threaten our team again."

"Yeah, a woman who we might know!"

"It's certainly complicated matters."

"They'll shit themselves."

"Possibly."

"I recognised him, my attacker. We saw him at some point yesterday."

"You didn't say that last night!"

"Didn't I?"

"No!"

"He was definitely familiar."

"Are you suggesting he might show up at the briefing this morning?"

"Or pull a sickie."

We're thinking aloud. I'd be studying every face in the room this morning. Sam would too. We'd also check on missing staff from today's rota, off duty staff. Sam and I were about to cause a buzz in Essex.

Looking at the clock, we only had thirty minutes before we'd be late.

"Kate, we need to arrange taking your evidence into Paddington Green. Would you call them to explain why we're not doing that first thing?"

"I need to speak to Jason Redruth, anyway."

Jason was Phil Andrews replacement – the new Detective Chief Inspector (DCI) and we hadn't spoken for a while.

Dialling the number from memory, they pick up on the second ring. Asking for Jason and stating my name I wait for his secretary, ready with my response to her.

"Oh, good morning. It's Katie-Ann Warwick here. Would you please let the Detective Chief Inspector know I'm on the phone with confidential information about our case, that he needs to hear direct from me. Thank you." Awaiting her response, I'm expecting resistance. Instead she informs me I'm on her list of calls to make this morning. That the man wants to talk to me!

Bombarding me with questions about my attack and the condition I'm in the man doesn't give me time to answer. Then he's out with what he really wants to ask: why hadn't I pressed Phil Andrews to contact Interpol?

Had they responded? Did he have information we weren't privy to?

"Just because there was only one e-mail, doesn't mean that's where I left it. I pressed him. The result was to split the department apart and have us re-assigned. Am I to assume something has materialised?" I say, as I place him on speaker.

"Indeed, you need to come in and that needs to be today. Should we say eleven thirty?"

"Sam and I can't do this morning, we're in the middle of something. That's why I've phoned you. The best we can do is call in when we drop the evidence off from the attack last night, but I can't give you a time on that."

"Okay, Sam can deal with the evidence and you can pop to my office and we'll talk. I'll hang about if you're late."

Returning to my conversation with Sam, he wants to know what I'm going to hand to Jason. My answer is simple. We have an image that Jodie has supplied. We've been manipulated – we've both seen her face before and need to know who she really is.

Sam, now composed and ready for the day ahead parks the car. Nobody would know how unbalanced he is, that the person they saw wore a protective mask. JJ had hinted at the scene something wasn't right and I wonder if Sam had spoken to him or if he'd just been more observant than me. I'd call him when I get the chance but wouldn't share anything private.

After signing in we're escorted into the building and through to the incident room. Fashionably late and fully aware how unusual this situation is we walk in expecting co-operation from a team who don't know who we are or who we work for – making trust a difficult task. Planning to make a convincing case for them to share what they know, I hope the sight of me will be motivational.

Our entrance stops conversation. All eyes are on me and the state of my face. Walking to the front of the room, Sam apologises for our lateness and continues to talk.

"Kate will explain her new look to you all in a moment. We are late because her apartment was turned over in the night and we had to wait for someone to arrive before we could leave." Allowing that to penetrate, he continues. "This case has taken its toll on both of us at different times. When one of us is targeted it effects the other. We ended up working together because of Carl Ashbeck, have both had our lives on the line because of him. Kate several times. I've lost my son because he killed him last year." Sam inhales deeply, "Now, I know Kate wants to talk to you, so I'll hand you over to her."

"Ashbeck and I have history." I begin. "Its personal. However, his rules have changed. We need you all to be vigilant. If you are involved in this case, consider yourself at risk. Last night I returned home, parked my car and was attacked a few paces from it." Looking around the room at the faces staring at me I scan each one for my attacker. "As you can see from my face my attacker was brutal. My bruising continues over my shoulders and back, my chest and ribs. My head is pounding. This wasn't Ashbeck in person but one of his gang members. How do I know this is connected? After my blouse was ripped open, he placed an ace of spades card inside my bra and told me to back of bitch." The room erupted with murmurings, but I wasn't done. "Be careful out there. Try not to be alone as his people are everywhere and they blend in, they watch and they pounce when you least expect it."

"Have you had yourself checked over?" Someone in front of me asked.

"No! She hasn't, Sam snapped. "Much to my disapproval."

"You shouldn't be left on your own with injuries like that. I hope you had someone with you last night."

"Yes, I did."

"Okay, make yourselves at home. Somebody needs to find Kate and Sam seats. I've got reports to share, although it's still early days so not much to go on yet. Firstly, I'm informed that Heidi, that's what we're calling our young witness, had a comfortable night and slept well. We'll not get daily reports but will hear from them if she shares new information relevant to our investigation. Contact will be once per week. This should help reduce the risk of interception. The times will be interchangeable and determined by her case worker. Sadie Kemp, her social worker, is preparing a report for us outlining her past, her relationship with the Collins family and prospect of adoption that has now been placed on hold. I've had dealings with Kemp, it will be detailed. Preliminary lab results are in. Ballistics are confirming a nine-millimetre pistol. We recovered matching ammunition from the female body and from the sofa behind the male body. The post-mortems were carried out by our usual team with the assistance of JJ, I believe some of you met him already. This investigation is a jurisdiction nightmare and the crossover between different authorities is going to prove essential if we're going to solve the case. I can't stress that enough. Sam and Kate are here to help and will answer your questions when they arise. Use their knowledge, its extensive.

"There won't be a press release, yet, despite them having noticed unusual activity about here.

"Okay, who else has something to offer this morning?"

"DNA has been pushed to urgent, guv. Another few days yet though," a voice from the edge of the room.

"Fingerprints lifted on the backdoor match the female victim," a woman at the back.

Information was forthcoming but nothing else significant had been released yet. It's still early days. Results take time. Sam and I shared my thoughts about my attacker with Karl, the gov, and he looked wide eyed at us. The thought that someone on his team might have connections both sides of this case astounded him.

"I hear you have a talent for sketching, you done that yet?"

Sam produces his notebook and opens it on the relevant page. Karl, sucking in air and shaking his head has a sudden panicked look about him.

"Follow me!"

Within three minutes we were outside a room, the door shut. Indicating to us to wait where we are, he burst through without knocking.

"Matty, I need a word."

"Sure, what's up?"

"Out here."

A few moments passed before the door frame was filled with a man whose face was familiar to me. Karl arrested him before letting him see me – and the resulting bruising of what he did to me last night. Ashbeck was infiltrating Essex police.

13

THE INSPECTOR CALLS

Jason Redruth sits at his desk. In front of him a brushed stainless-steel nameplate reminds anyone who visits his office of his importance – Detective Chief Inspector. He'd had his work cut out when he arrived having replaced Phil Andrews who had bought shame on this department. His briefing on the Ashbeck case had provided initial insight into the complexity of how so many people high up in the organisation had yielded to Ashbeck's wishes. Not only was it his job to locate this escaped prisoner it was his mission to raise morale among his staff.

Hidden in his top draw, removed from evidence was Rachel Smith's mobile phone. Kept permanently charged he wanted to know who tried to contact her and what their business was. A select few had been entrusted with the knowledge of his endeavours – but only because he needed them to chase up each lead for him. After two months of silence, the phone had suddenly leapt back into action today.

Something was happening, at last.

Greg Kingston. The name came to his immediate attention. A troublesome chap he'd not been able to pin a crime to yet as he'd always been too careful. What was a woman of Rachel Smith's standing doing with his number? If, indeed, it was the same man. Having his name appear in yet one more investigation was reason enough for a visit – one he'd make himself.

By rights, he should be passing this information onto the private investigation team. In his eyes they were a break-away unit with their own rules and possibly their own agenda. He didn't care so much for the past results they claim to have achieved. What mattered to him, was that they were failing now. Months had passed, and nobody was any closer to the re-capture of Ashbeck. Three weeks ago, he'd decided to stem the flow of information coming from his department – not that there'd been any so far. Something didn't feel right to him.

Drawing a crude grid on the pad in front of him, he writes the names of the team and makes notes beside them, highlighting what he likes and dislikes about each person. Spending ten minutes on each, he has a comprehensive list once finished. He decides that Kate is the most approachable and that he'll focus his attention on her. Despite this, he won't make it easy for her – she will have to earn his respect and the information he will share, if any.

The last thing I needed was another meeting – I'm exhausted. When the Detective Chief Inspector wants to talk about a case you're working together, you do have to put yourself out. There's an unspoken rule of commitment and he's hung about for me today. I owe him some respect. Heading along the corridor, I take more pain relief and wash it down with a little plastic cup of water from the cooler I'd just passed. Lack of food wasn't helping matters.

Greeting me at the door of his department he makes a fuss of the state of my face as so many people had done today. The bruising was really beginning to show now – I'd taken a look in the visor mirror before getting out of the car.

Getting down to the reason for our meeting, Jason Redruth is out with what he has on his mind, a repeat of his earlier question.

"Why didn't you push for Interpol's involvement in the original Ashbeck case?"

"My original request was declined. I questioned Phil Andrews about it and his response was to re-shuffle the department. A codeword was assigned to the case and nobody allowed to speak of it. What was I supposed to do?"

"Fight it, contact them yourself. Do something, Kate." He looks at me. "Here, I've taken a copy for you but please be careful who you show it to. I'm not convinced that everyone in this investigation can be trusted."

"There's only one person in this investigation I trust fully," I state with my eye contact never faltering.

"Sam?"

"Me." I say, matter-of-factly.

The DCI leans back in his chair with both eyebrows raised and his fingers interlinked across his chest. I hope I just earnt a little respect from him.

"What makes you say that?"

"It's simple. We should have solved this case by now. Someone is withholding information and that's not me. I'm ninety nine percent sure it's not Sam either. We are the only two people investigating Ashbeck to come under attack. He knows to focus on us, why is that?"

"You have a point."

"We've arrested the man who assaulted me last night. He worked at police headquarters, in Essex." Jason Redruth was stunned. "He infiltrates everywhere!"

"Yes, he does. In the report I've given you Interpol have shared possible links to some dated murders. They linked these cases a long time ago. However, they remain unsolved. Given the details we've supplied they are re-opening their investigations. We've been given a name. I've double checked the data. I know you have access to higher clearance and I'd appreciate you taking a look."

"Are there links to Vietnam?"

"How do you know that?"

"Speculation, on Sam's part. We've made searches, but they came up blank. That doesn't mean we've dismissed it. Maybe it's time you saw for yourself our research. Perhaps you could meet Sam and I this evening?"

"You have my attention, Ms Warwick. What time?"

We make the arrangements before I head out to find Sam.

"We'll tell you what we've found out together." I say as I walk out his door with the envelope tucked securely under my arm.

Jason Redruth knocks on the front door of Greg Kingston's

home. Without a search warrant it can only be an informal chat but as his name has just materialised he wants his presence known. When there's no answer he looks around for a hidden camera but cannot see one. Scowling, he retreats and vanishes around the corner, his shoulders hunched against the cold.

Greg Kingston sits in his kitchen with a cup of tea watching his CCTV monitor. The call he placed to Rachel Smith's phone earlier obviously ended up on Redruth's desk. Knowing which Murder Investigation Team (MIT) he will be up against when the lady calls him will be helpful and the daft ape has just given himself away.

14

HOPE IN HELL

Certain he was being kept underground, Max Smith felt he deserved the life he now had. At the time of his marriage to Rachel their vows had meant everything. Over the years something had shifted in him and she wasn't enough. He'd yearned for more than his beautiful wife could ever be expected to give. Rachel deserved better than him, yet he couldn't let her go. His perverted lust for what is forbidden alongside his obsession with the man who provided the women had led him here. Women who knew no boundaries who allowed him to sin against them had led him here too. Ultimately, he took full responsibility for his behaviour – he was remorseful.

Conditions were squalid. Sitting on the filthy mattress he envisioned the broken woman Rachel would now be. Of her struggling with their younger daughter and her mood swings, and of the new son he'd never met. He'd always wanted a son and was destined never to meet him. His eldest daughter was strong. Images of her holding the family together were keeping him going.

Running his filthy hands through his dirty hair he knew he'd not recognise himself if he was to see his reflection. His hair was the longest he'd known it to be and his face now adorned a beard and moustache. Without the opportunity to wash, his body was prone to skin sores that wouldn't heal. Cleansing them with his drinking water the best he could was saving them from infection, so far.

Several times, the urge not to drink or eat the soup-like food they bought to him had been strong. To allow his body to drift into unconsciousness and then into death – yet something made him carry on. Perhaps it was the pain dehydration gave him – the feeling his head would split in two – maybe it was something entirely different. Deep down he believed he could right his wrong and become accountable for his actions. He needed to apologise – not just to his family – but to the city of London too.

The thought of slipping away in this hell-hole and being left to rot was unappealing. Hanging onto slim hope that Rachel was looking for him, to welcome him back into her arms was keeping him alive for now.

15

SHARK

Rachel Smith has settled for life in a small Essex city. Far enough from London to be out of the way and unrecognised but close enough not to be out of touch and in on the action when needed. Chelmsford was home for now.

Wearing her hair extremely short she owned several wigs giving her a variety of looks and the ability to blend into any situation. This decision had been an easy one considering her situation and her new working conditions. Her survival depended upon blending in and hiding from the people who might be looking for her.

Family life had always been important. Protecting her children her priority and responsibility. No longer the quiet, respected wife of the deputy commissioner she now has a reputation.

A money lender.

Employing debt collectors, she's tripled her money in three months. With the help of Chris, the now ex police officer who helped deliver her baby with her eldest daughter the night her family had been held captive in their own home, she'd become unstoppable.

Having been placed in the witness protection programme, she'd broken away to take control of her own destiny. Surrounding herself with the very type of people the police were trying to protect her from, she'd never felt so safe.

Chris thinks he's keeping her and her entire family secure but what he doesn't realise is there's a second person keeping an eye on them too. He'd burst into their lives, gun in hand, and wrestled her eldest daughter to the floor because she'd tried to attack him – she thought the armed response team had come to kill them not save them. After the new baby had been delivered, the pair were inseparable. They'd bonded.

Unsure if she could trust a man who'd worked for the police, after discovering what her husband had been up to, she was dubious. So far, Chris seemed loyal – but yet to earn her respect. She needs time to establish where his allegiance lays. Could he be feeding information back to his old colleagues? Mindful of this she was careful to only give him responsibilities that would implement him in the illegal activities they were involved in.

Chris had no idea of the full implications of what her plans were.

Chris had, however stood by the family. Provided for them while things were tough in the beginning and was loyal and devoted to Jane. He doted on her. He'd also provided some useful contacts – people he'd heard about from being in the force – she hoped they never found out he was a copper for they would slice him apart.

Initially shocked and intimidated by the world she was rising in, her determination to thrive and dominate now shone through. Money was only one side of what she had planned. The underground scene had awakened a dark side to her. A maliciousness that bubbled under her surface she was eager to enforce.

Chris didn't know about this secret of hers, of the hate that was brewing and how cold her heart was becoming. Tracing her husband would be the start. Word on the street was he'd been taken to the New Forest. She'd sent one of her contacts there to trace him. So far there'd been no response. After four days of waiting her impatience snagged at her mind and the urge to pick up the phone was strong. She knew better. Cool and professional distance was required despite her anxious need for information.

Deciding she needed to venture out she opts for a business suit and long, straight hair. Gluing her wig in place, she pins the hair back into a sleek style. Slipping into high heels, she sneaks down the stairs and tiptoes towards the front door hoping to make it before anyone notices – space and some quiet time is needed this morning.

Chris, always alert and on her heels, is beside her before she's able to escape. Her two daughters continue their education in another part of the home and her young son is with his nanny in another. Ensuring the door is locked behind them, Rachel and Chris venture outside.

"Where 'we heading to?"

"Just needed to escape these walls. Some space."

"Space from me also?"

"I'm a grown woman, I'd like to be able to walk along the high street alone."

"You're a wanted woman. I'm here to protect you. It's best I tag along. You know that."

"It's frustrating."

"That's life."

Jane Smith hears a mobile ringing and rushes to answer it. Knowing her mother has just left with Chris and that she's waiting on news of her father. Information has been flimsy. Grabbing the phone and swiping the screen she answers as per her brief and speaks clearly,

"Hello, you're through to City Personal. Please proceed with details of your mission," and awaited the response.

Even if the contact realised it wasn't Rachel, they knew to pass on the information. That the person they were speaking to was to be trusted. She wasn't allowed to write anything down. Remembering the information was vital. With her heart pumping fast, she listened intently to the male voice and knew the details that she was receiving could bring her father home. He was alive! Excitement filled her heart and overwhelmed her. Ending this call, she used her own phone to ring Chris. Her voice catching slightly, she demanded they both return home immediately and that she'd have the room set up for a meeting. This was code that her younger sister, Maisy would be out the way.

Feeling panicked, Rachel spun around with Chris following as he always did. Rushing towards home, her first fear was the safety of her three children. Since being held hostage, images of that night haunted her – closing her eyes at night giving her flashbacks of the three of them being tied to chairs. Surrounding herself with the harshness of the underground world she somehow feels that she's found a way to rise above what's happened. That the harsh world she now inhibits provides her with a safety net of protection against the people who might want harm to come of her. Yet moments such as these put her on edge, as her motherly instinct kicks in. Having Jane involved is the last thing she wants.

Jane had set up the table and ensured Maisy and the baby were entertained at the opposite end of the house. When Rachel and Chris walked in the room, it was obvious Jane felt she had some kind of leverage over her mother – a chance to establish some high ground. Having chosen to head the table, which in her mother's eyes was disrespectful she now hung her head in shame. Defiance streaked through her when she refused to move on Chris's request.

Unbeknown to Jane, Rachel had two sides. When pushed during the course of her new role a darkness emerges that she'd rather keep from her family. Despite this, venom escapes from her mouth.

"If you're playing with big game you learn respect. Move!" Her tone stern, with eyes fixed on her daughter she moves to the head of the table and leans against the back of the chair to begin her interrogation as Jane slips from her seat, almost cowering, and takes up her new position opposite Chris.

"You'd better have good reason to call me back."

Not knowing if she dared to look at her mother, Jane decides to direct her answer at Chris. Looking him in the eye she speaks as clearly as she can with a confidence she doesn't feel,

"Your secret phone rang," she announced before pausing for effect. "I answered it the way you told me to." She had her mother's attention. Silence fell in the room as anticipation of her next comment built.

"Dad has been located, co-ordinates will follow but I need to ask something first."

"Jane I will answer your questions but please let's give Chris the coordinates first. He can get the wheels in motion, so we can get to your father."

Feeling the burn of tears behind her eyelids she felt compelled to share what she knew and immediately regretted doing so when her mother left the room without giving her any answers. She'd looked the locations up herself and knew her father was in the New Forest, although had no idea why he would be there.

Chris promised Jane he'd talk with her later and chased after Rachel who was fuming. The one time she'd left the phone behind it had rung and Jane now knew her father was still alive – making what Rachel had planned look very suspicious now. Unbeknown to her, Chris was fully aware of her plans even though she thought she had managed to keep them from him.

16

PERIL

Having met with the prison guard without Kate, Sam decides to send her a report rather than phoning her, knowing how angry she'll be. That aside, he's also returned to Maldon. Resuming his search for Ashbeck.

Phoning ahead, he's re-booked into the same bed and breakfast as before. Walking into the bar, the landlady greets him with a broad smile and a food menu and pouring him a pint of larger before fetching him the guest book to sign – which he does in the name he used when he went undercover last year with Kate – James Peterson.

Selecting what has become his usual seat, he sits drinking his pint and reading from the menu before returning to the bar to order food and to collect his room key. Heading up the familiar stairs, thankful for the same room as before.

Deciding he didn't need to unpack, he selected clean clothes from his backpack, grabbed his toiletries and headed for the bathroom. He needed a quick shower before he ate, to wash the smell of the prison from him. After dinner, and once she'd had a chance to read the report, he'd phone Kate.

Once back in the bar, he settled back into his seat with a new pint just in time for his meal to be delivered: steak and ale pie, chips and peas. Tucking in and enjoying his meal Sam surveyed his surroundings, clocking a man staring at him, a bandanna tied low on his head. Remaining calm, and finishing his food before returning his plate to the bar, Sam is almost inaudible as he asks, with a raised eyebrow,

"Bandanna man. Is he a regular?"

"Never seen him before," she says holding eye contact "but he's freaking me out."

Turning to face the man who's been staring at him just in time to see him disappear out the door he rushes out in time to see his silhouette vanish around the corner. Chasing ghosts in a strange town's not ideal, especially after dark, but he finds himself jumping the gate into a churchyard. Graves line the pathway and halogen spotlights illuminate the church, plunging the grounds into darkness.

Three paces in someone grabs him from behind, an arm wrapping around his neck, pulling him to the ground. Fire explodes in his back as blade penetrates below his shoulder blade. Letting out a curdling scream, he struggles to get free from the man's grip and onto his feet. Face to face, the two men lock eyes.

Sam Cooper and Carl Ashbeck meet at last.

Plunging forwards, Sam throws a punch, making impact with Ashbeck's jaw. His right arm useless, he attempts another shot with his left. Ashbeck, backing off, heads towards the gate and away leaving Sam lunging into thin air. Staggering forwards, and stumbling, he crashes to the ground in pain.

Knowing he needs to find help quickly he starts to edge his way towards the gate. Lying here wasn't an option, not if he wanted to survive. Using his good arm, he levered himself up and leant on the gate for support. Taking deep breaths, he swung his body over and, careful not to touch the knife on anything, landed the other side. Using the church wall for support, he slowly moves towards the pub, blood trickling each time he moves. Those few metres took forever and the last of his strength.

Somehow he finds the energy he needs and doesn't collapse until he's burst through the pub door, the knife still lodged in his back. Rushing to his side, the landlady is shouting,

"Get that thing out of him!"

"No!" Sam manages to say, "leave it." Taking shallow breaths before he continues. "Remove it and I'll bleed to death in minutes. Get my phone, it's in my room," he demands. No energy for manners.

"Dial nine-nine-nine, we need an ambulance!" She demands, as she leaves.

"Already on its way."

Disappearing, she fumbles on the waistband of her jeans for her key fob before heading up the stairs. When she returns, phone in hand, she presents it to Sam, demanding his fingerprint.

"Ring Princess. Tell her to meet me at the hospital." He says, his breaths becoming too shallow, "then lock the phone."

Having organised what I believe Sam might need for his hospital stay and a few things for myself, I grab my keys from the kitchen table. Ensuring the door to the spare bedroom – our incident room – is secure, I head out and make my way to the car. Uneasiness spreads through me as I step out the lift and scan the area, making a dash for the car and lock myself inside. Quick to start the engine and move away, I add underground car parks to the list of anxiety evoking locations. Having pre-set the navigation system on my phone, I pause at the exit of the car park to enable the Bluetooth before pulling onto the road.

Unable to stay angry at Sam for visiting the prison without me, I'm now frantically worried he might die from his injuries. Processing what he'd told me about his conversation with the prison guard was helping to keep me focussed, however. Apparently, Ashbeck had become fascinated with the illuminati early on after his incarceration. He'd found a book in the library and checked it out numerous times. After his escape they'd found notes in his room on certain passages from the book. Owls featured heavily – especially the Minerva owl. He also made hints that he intended to create his own God and start to worship it. Kerry had been the one to interview the guard, if she was privy to this information she hadn't shared it with us.

Sam had requested Ashbeck's visitor's log, which had already been supplied despite us not having seen it. I was now wondering how much information Kerry withheld from us. Something wasn't sitting right with how our boss was operating. What was her agenda? My views would be heard about this – how could the case move forward if we were not presented with all the evidence?

Jason Redruth would be one of the first people I would contact with the new information. Now that I'd opened a channel of communication with him, I was keen to keep it open.

Having parked and fed coins into the metre I break into a

run, eager to be by Sam's side. Heading for the emergency department I show my identification and explain who I am here to see. The fact I'm escorted through to a family room immediately doesn't give me much faith in his condition. Two police officers are already waiting in the room, with an evidence bag on the table in front of them. Seeing me eye it, one of them removes it and places it on the floor behind his feet.

Knowing that Sam arrived with a knife in his back, it would mean he was out of surgery if that was what was in the bag. My hands immediately start shaking at the thought. Please God, don't let him be dead.

"Are you here with Sam Cooper? What's your name?"

After providing identification, they were more relaxed and open with me. Explaining that a nurse had popped in to tell them he was out of surgery and that the surgeon would be along just as soon as he could.

Sam was alive. Looking upwards, I silently mouth *"thank you"* and hope that I've been heard.

"Is that the knife in the bag?"

"No, no. Sam's clothes. We've not been given the knife yet."

"This is going to seem like a strange request but I'm going to need photos of it," I say, smiling sweetly and in hope that they won't put up a fight.

"It's okay, you two come with a warning. We're 'ere coz a crime's bin committed on our patch. We have to evidence everything, take it to our station and then we have to share the info with your division. You can 'ave your pics."

"Thanks. I wish the surgeon would hurry up, I just want to see Sam."

"We've been here the entire time. There might be quite a wait before you can see him."

"He'll be out the door as soon as he can stand, I'll guarantee that."

They both smile at me, not believing my words as the door opens. Spinning round, I'm greeted to a man dressed in green scrubs flanked by two nurses. Exhaustion emits from all their faces and tension begins to work its way through my body as I face the words he is about to speak.

"Katie-Ann Warwick?"

"Yes, that's me," I say nervously. "How is Sam doing?"

"He's a lucky man. The operation was a success. The blade was buried deeply but it has missed all major tendons. There is bone damage and we need to be mindful of infection, but I've patched him up the best I can. He'll have one more scar to add to his portfolio. Mr Cooper is already awake and trying to get out of bed."

Smiling, I can barely contain my excitement that the operation was over, successful and that he's already awake.

"I know you two are trouble, the most part of Mr Cooper's file is locked and look at the state of your face! If you come with me, I'll take a look at it before you go and see him. You walk in here black and blue, with bruises a day or so old with a cut above your eye and your partner gets stabbed. I've checked your name on our database too, your file is also locked. Who are you?"

"What we're into, is on a need to know basis but I can show you my ID." I'm smiling as I hand it over to him.

"You don't think I need to know, after saving Sam?"

"Trust me, you're better not knowing."

"You're probably right, but even so!"

"Someone at our HQ knows who you two are," the younger police officer interrupts, "apparently, you've met him already.

We're under strict instructions to look after you."

"We know your partner was the first person our pathologist phoned after an autopsy the other day," the younger one says, tapping his nose with an index finger. "People talk."

"People need to be careful."

Silence fell, and I rummage in my bag for a bottle of water.

Stepping into the corridor the surgeon, I now know as Stuart, and I walk towards Sam's room. He's agreed to take me straight to him and to look at my wound there. Deciding to give him a little detail, now we were alone, I pander to his desire to be let in.

"We're working on a high-profile case, that's particularly complex. The fact we've both been attacked means we're closing in on something large. Sam will check himself out as soon as he can stand up, I do need to warn you of that. Having him here will compromise the safety of your other patients and he will not stay."

Stuart looked at me in disbelief, took hold of my arm and we stopped walking.

"I have a care of duty to every single patient, Sam included. You understand?"

"I get that, and if you knew what we were up against you'd understand."

"Try me!"

Continuing to walk, he dutifully opens doors for me as we negotiate the maize of corridors that eventually lead us to

Sam's private room. Having stopped at a desk first to arrange what he needs to fix my head we make our way towards Sam's private room. Laying face-down on the bed, his head at the foot end its obvious Sam has been up and about. Rushing to him, I embrace him the best I can.

"Let me get up, I need a proper hug, Princess."

"You're not supposed to be out of bed, Mr Cooper!"

"Rules, rules, rules!" He says with raised eyebrows as he manoeuvres himself so he's sitting on the edge of the bed, we wrap our arms around each other. Mindful of his wound I embrace him with one hand on his head and slide the other down his back. Having forgotten about my sore muscles and grazes in his drugged state, I fail to mention them as he grips onto me and allows me to feel the fear he has.

Gradually he releases his hold.

"Oh, I'm hurting you. I'm so sorry." He holds me at arm's length. "Sorry," he repeats.

"It's okay."

"While we're here, please get yourself looked at. It's becoming infected."

"Stuart has kindly offered."

"Stuart?"

"Your surgeon."

"Just waiting for the trolley to arrive and I'll have it sorted. I was met with resistance at the front desk, but I won through with my charming smile."

Unable to rest Sam is up and in the shower while his surgeon attends to my face. Inserting a needle and drawing puss from my wound, I'm startled how much poison he is removing. No wonder it's been itching for the past few hours. Unsure if its pain or relief I'm feeling, but aware it's making me feel light headed, I steady myself with my hands despite the fact I'm sitting. Scraping the wound with a scalpel, to reopen the wound before applying stitches, he makes a neater job than I had allowed the night of the attack.

Sam emerges from the wet room, dressed from the waist down and his wound dressing in his hand. With a sheepish look on his face he bins it and turns to show me the damage. It's more impressive than the look on Stuart's face.

Having checked himself out of hospital we were now nearing the pub where Sam had been staying. His car remained parked nearby and needed collecting. Under the influence of anaesthetic for forty-eight hours, I'd confiscated his car keys and would hand them to the landlady as she sounded formidable. I'd stay the night but needed to get away early in the morning.

Walking through the door, Sam receives a warm welcome and loud cheers.

"Whoop! Whoop!" One-man cheers.

"Oggy! Oggy! Oggy!"

"Oi! Oi! Oi!" Echoes from somewhere else in the room.

The woman, I assume is the landlady makes a dash towards Sam.

"They can't have let you out already, James. It's not even twenty-four hours yet!"

James? He's not told me we're undercover.

"This is Lori," he's quick to add. "My better half."

Unphased by my appearance, seats are cleared, and space made.

"Your usual?"

"Hadn't better, coke please."

"And for you, love?"

"Same, please." I say.

"Martin, take over for a bit please." The landlady demands, as she brings our drinks over, with a pint of ale for herself.

"What happened to you, Princess?" She surprised me with her choice of names.

Sam and I both shot her a look.

"You presented me with your index finger and asked me to call Princess. How else do you think she ended up at the hospital?"

"I don't remember that!"

"I assumed that was the hospital calling!" I say, "thank you," I add quickly.

"Whatever shit you two have bought to my door, thank you. You've tripled my trade." Smiling, before she adds "nothing like a stabbing to bring folk out about here. Now drink up, you both look like death, then go and get some rest."

Doing as we'd been told, for once, Sam had led me to the room. Stripping, folding his clothes and heading for the shower, I follow and watch as he prizes off his wound dressing for the second time today. Twenty-four hours ago, he was taking care of me – now it's my turn.

I was beginning to think this case would be the end of the pair of us.

17

FACING REALITY

The house was no longer being processed by the police, of that she was sure. Having spent the last two days watching it herself, from a safe distance, the only activity had been the occasional passing car.

Using her own key, Shadow sneaks back in through the back door and, once again, moves about under the cover of darkness. The sound of her high heeled boots echoing through the hallway. For a few seconds she lingers in the lounge doorway, remembering. Goosebumps prickle her skin. Despite having killed before, it had never been personal: this felt different and she was unable to remove it from her mind.

Returning to search in the safe for documentation that would identify herself and also her sister, she needed to get a grip. Protecting her sister wasn't paramount, but the need to cover her own identity a major concern: distancing herself, legally, from any connection at this point in her life a requirement for survival. Refocusing on the task at hand, she makes her way towards the portrait dominating the hallway: the oil image of some ancestor who's name she didn't care to remember that takes pride of place above the table. Lifting what looks like a heavy guilt frame from its brackets she removes the lightweight fake frame and places it against the bannisters to reveal the family safe. Now all she needed was some luck – after all these years, would the code be the same?

Holding her breath, she keyed in the numbers and listened as the digits clicked, one by one: three-six-two-four. She'd never found the relevance of these numbers, but knew they'd mean something to her father. To her knowledge, he never knew she'd learned the code. The door released. As she opened it wide, it squeaked. With a pounding heart her search begins: rifling through her father's belongings felt intrusive. She'd done it so many times before as an act of defiance – her way of taking back a little control when she was younger. This time felt different. Death had a way of changing things, but she hadn't expected to feel guilt.

Her left hand suddenly touched something that intrigued her: a leather-bound book. Pulling it out for further inspection, she gently opened the fragile cover and turned the torch from her mobile on, so she could see it.

Horrified, she reads the first entry, then second and the third, tears free-falling as she does. Each entry about her, what he'd done, how he forced her to partake and, ultimately detested but couldn't resist her. That guilt fuelled his very existence and that he deserved to be shot.

Shot. She had given him what he wanted. The bastard – he'd had the final say. No wonder he'd just sat there and let it happen. A feeling came over her that she hadn't experienced in many years: an emptiness filled with such pain and sorrow and the need for release, to expel fear. Rushing to the kitchen she searches for a knife – the overpowering need to cut her flesh taking control of her mind.

Pushing her glove down and her jacket up she bares a small part of her arm and puts pressure onto her skin. A feeling of anticipation begins to spread through her at the thought of the promised release but she can't go through with it now. Dropping the knife into the sink, she covers her arm over. Her body gives an involuntary shudder.

Stepping back to the safe, she places the diary in her pocket and continues to search, it had to be here: seconds ticked by as time stood still.

Finally, she came across it: the little folder. Perfect.

Returning the portrait onto its brackets, she retraced her steps back through the kitchen.

The cutting – the pain and bleeding it caused – had taken her to a place she felt in control. Although this sense of control was only brief: the more she cut the more she needed to continue with the cycle she'd created. The more she indulged herself in the joy of her secret the more she needed to feel it. Before long the rare occasion became weekly, then daily – some days more often. She had needed help.

Both parents knew what was happening. How could they not know – how could he not know – he saw the wounds every night when he visited her in her bed. Her mother peeked her head through the crack in the door before she quietly closed it each night – she saw the guilty look in her eyes as the light extinguished on her dignity, her childhood, her rights and her sanity. It made her as bad as him.

The day she turned fifteen things changed: a feeling deep inside, low down in her tummy, like bubbles popping. Of course, she had no idea what this meant until her belly started to swell months later, and real movements could be felt from within – she was carrying her father's child.

Distraught, frightened and repulsed by her messed up world, she made her decision.

Having selected her favourite object – her pen lid she'd sharpened with a knife – she made her way to the family bathroom and locked the door. While the water ran into the bath, she undressed and eased herself into the hot water. As tears streaked down her pale cheeks she sliced open both wrists and place her arms into the water.

She was ready. Accepting.

Unsure of how much time had passed she came around to her mother gathering her in her arms. Tears were falling freely and when she spoke her voice was almost inaudible.

"I'm so sorry my darling."

Sirens were approaching and when she woke the next time she was in hospital. Apparently, she couldn't leave. The expression 'sectioned' wasn't something she'd heard of before – whatever it was – it had happed to her.

For all of her mother's faults, she had finally stepped up and saved her, but the damage was done. At seven months pregnant she remained in hospital for therapy and for the birth. When her daughter was born she didn't want to hold it – or even look at it – she signed the adoption papers immediately.

Her sister had made contact and was visiting regularly and promised her a better life. She promised stability, love, support, and education. Finally, when she was well enough to leave hospital it was her sister and her husband who collected her, took her in and protected her. They introduced her to their beautiful daughter who was so full of love. The two bonded immediately and became inseparable.

To this day neither know the truth: that they are mother and daughter.

The effect her abuse has had on her life and choices has led her into a double life. Her parents had ruined her life and they were now allowed to foster. That was cruel. Her sister refused to help her deal with that over the years, instead choosing to erase their existence because she could.

Both girls had been suffocated, emotionally, in this house. Friendships at school were non-existent – the burdens of their life so heavy on their shoulders that any form of social life wasn't possible. Developmental issues were, understandably, highlighted and dismissed. Their parents couldn't risk having friends around in case a body showed up.

Mindful she'd been using her torch, Shadow was keen to make a hasty exit – police presence had diminished but the neighbours may be watching. If someone had seen a light, they may dial nine-nine-nine.

Documentation and journal tucked inside her jacket, along with her trusted gun, she makes her way out the back door, through the gate and mounts her bike. As the engine comes to life she makes sure to rev it as loudly as possible – the one hundred and ninety-nine horse power engine roars as she makes her way down the road – the neighbours will, no doubt, be wondering what has just occurred. The curtains will be twitching and the woman over the road will notice the back gate is open when it was closed earlier.

There was no doubt in Shadow's mind that the police would be called, but it was too late. The evidence connecting her to the house had vanished.

Riding the BMW made her feel energised in a way that nothing else could match and she had enjoyed the journey back to the city. Using her key fob to release the gate, it opens inwards to reveal a small courtyard, just large enough to ride her bike into and be able to turn it around. Parking, she pats her jacket on both sides feeling for her gun, the documents and journal. Content all is in order she enters the property through the side door. The doorman nods his greeting but does not attempt to search her. He will watch her bike and knows she doesn't intend to be in the building for long because she has left it out. Slipping past him without a word, she glances around. All looks to be in order – the bar is busy with customers. She works her way towards the bar: when she reaches it, there is no need for conversation. As soon as she is noticed her usual is placed before her. Smiling, she nods. No money changes hands.

This lady has special privileges here.

It isn't long until she has company and drinks are flowing. He doesn't realise what a dangerous game he's playing. Within ten minutes they move into a more private area, with seating. The barman delivers a pitcher of mojito and two glasses and leaves the pair to their own devices. The lighting is purposely discrete here and within a couple of minutes the man knows what's expected of him. No names are exchanged.

He doesn't need names – he knows exactly who she is. Sex hadn't been part of the mission but getting close had and he'd go to any lengths to get the job done.

With an intensity in her eyes, parted lips and a firm touch, she begins to massage his thigh, gradually moving higher and higher. She doesn't usually notice features but this one is stunning. Tall, well over six feet, with blonde hair pulled back into a pony tail. She estimated him to be in his late twenties. His eyes were an amazing shade of blue giving his eyes an intensity she liked. His stubble about two days old. Dressed in jeans and a tight-fitting black shirt, that showed his figure, a gold chain showing beneath it.

Shifting in his seat slightly he slips one arm behind her and the other on her leg. He slides his hand up and down her leather trousers, getting higher and higher with each upward stroke. Their eyes were locked. Leaving their drinks on the table, she grabs his arm and leads him through the busy bar towards a door and into a corridor.

Pushing him against the wall, Shadow presses herself against his firm body. There's no time to explore flesh, she requires her needs to be met instantly tonight. Grabbing at his belt, she hastily unbuckles it and unbuttons his jeans before reaching inside her jacket to produce a condom. Handing it over, she leaves him to deal with it while she unzips her leather trousers. Grabbing her, he pulls her close and kisses her passionately, before spinning her around and pushing her, face-first against the wall. Placing her hands in front of her face, she allows him to push her trousers down. Parting her legs slightly, she feels his hardness sliding between her cheeks a few times, teasing her. When he enters, she lets out a loud moan. Taking hold of her hips he thrusts deeply until she can't take any more.

Releasing her, he spins her around, kisses her gently, removes the condom and tucks himself away. He didn't release himself, but he'd just learnt a lot about his client.

The night was only just beginning for Shadow. There was something else on her mind now she walked back through the door, re-adjusting her clothing. She didn't usually let them live after sex but this one, she liked. Looking for him in the bar, she hoped he'd still be around, but she couldn't see him. Maybe he'd gone into the gents.

Sex with the blonde stranger had captivated her and she'd allowed him to gain control: a rarity on her part. Now feeling compelled to regain the balance she always needs – murder is on her mind.

Returning to her bike she rides through the streets of London until she finds a quiet location: a tree lined residential area. Her mind focused on what she needs to do she parks her bike and disappears around the back of the property.

Breaking the glass with a garden ornament before reaching inside to unlock the door triggers the alarm system. She'd have to work quickly. Annoyed with herself for not noticing this house was compromised she moves boldly and swiftly through the kitchen, retrieving her gun from her pocket. The lounge light is on and the door open. She heads towards it and arrives in time to see a woman disappearing behind the sofa and a man trying to follow. Aiming her gun, she fires a single shot, the sound vibrating through the room that hits him in the head.

His body, jerking forwards and away from the blast smashes against the wall before slipping towards the floor. The woman screams and tries to run from behind the safety of her hiding place. Shadow shoots her in the left knee and watches her as she crashes to the floor in agony. Dragging herself along, her blood spilling onto the cream carpet, the woman refuses to give up her fight. Firing two more times, once in the stomach and another head shot, Shadow smiles as she watches the life drain from her eyes. From her top pocket she removes two ace of spades playing cards and tears them in half: one for each of the bodies.

Returning to the kitchen, she places her gun on the table and walks out the door and towards her bike. The alarm, still ringing in her ears will be attracting attention and she needed to place as much distance as possible between this place and herself.

As she pulls out the end of the road, she notices police cars arriving in the distance – their blue flashing lights illuminating the night sky. Unprepared to hang around, she opens the throttle and heads North.

She has business to attend in Scotland.

18

EVOLUTION

Ritual has become a vital part of Ashbeck's existence.

During his time inside prison, he'd established a forced routine he now found hard to break. Within that time, he factored his new-found obsession of symbolism into this routine without much effort, managing to establish patterns where he needed to: counting numbers of bricks, within the numbering system he'd discovered, for example.

Spending hours meditating and reading each day had kept him out of trouble and his mind free of the evil forces that had driven him from such a young age. Prison appeared, on the surface, to be good for him. Yet he was being enabled through his obsessions: his obsession with owls emerged early – the more he read about their importance the more focus he gave them. Their initial appeal to him was in their connection to dead bodies: the old custom of leaving the deceased at home with a candle by their bed at night. Learning that the owls were attracted by the insects gathering because of the light at the window drew him in: when it was revealed to him that they were not there to feed upon the insects but to collect the souls of the dead he was captivated.

From there he was drawn towards the Illuminati order and their symbolism. Within a month his whole organisation had been re-arranged and tiered in such a way that mirrored this organisation. The use of symbolism became important to Ashbeck to the point of obsession and to the new way of his thinking. It was providing him with the protection he'd only dreamed about before and enabled him to utilise many top officials without them realising what or who they were getting involved with.

In celebration he'd had two owl eyes tattooed onto his forehead, his only step out of line during his incarceration, his escape excluded. The owl, the sign of rationality and intellectualism was a permanent reminder to all beneath him that he was the head of his organisation and not to be crossed. His tattoos were now, however a hindrance and his biggest regret.

Since escaping, and despite continuing with meditation, his evil urges were bubbling to the surface. He could feel both his mood and impulses shifting. Having selected a new victim that delighted him, he was thrilled that he didn't have to go anywhere to watch her.

The strawberry blond lived next door and he was looking forward to spending some special time with her. Before that could happen, there were some extraordinary preparations he needed to carry out in his cellar.

Peeping through the curtains to make sure it was dark, Ashbeck decided now was a good time to venture outside. Taking the large, rusty key from the window ledge he exits the back door and keeps close to the side of the house. The cellar door is only four metres away. The four steps down are steep. Stopping at the bottom, he inserts the old key into the lock of the wooden door, turning it he pushes hard with his shoulder: the door gives with a groan and he slips inside, quickly closing it behind him. The cold, damp air hit his senses, and he welcomes it. The wet earthy smell reminds him of his time in the jungles of Vietnam and of his friend, the Sergeant. The two men, bonding in their hatred towards women and in their torture and humiliation of their platoon if they didn't conform to their methods of war. Smiling in the darkness at his memories, he reaches inside his pocket to pull out his lighter and sparks the flame into life. Before him is a table he's set up and he walks towards it. Eleven candles are lined up along the length of it. He lights each in turn.

They represent his vision.

Dropping to his knees he prays to the dead owl he keeps on the table in front of the candles before beginning an hour of meditation.

Once his body is at one with his mind he begins the preparations. Over the past few weeks he's been collecting what he needs. Just a short walk from his home is a hospital, and he's been sneaking in undetected and stealing from the stores and has everything he needs now. With just the set-up to organise, his plans are coming together, ready for his transformation.

Praying to the owl is his own twist on what he's created. He'd taken its life and he believed this gave him power. Giving daily thanks to the owl, in Ashbeck's head, was strengthening his mind for what lay ahead for him.

19

THE BOSS

Convinced I'd just heard a fist pound on my front door I hurry to dry myself. Any relaxing effect of my shower fast wearing off. Ruffling my fingers through my short hair, I throw clothes on in haste before rushing to place my eye against the spy hole.

Kerry Preston was standing the other side. My boss was flanked by a team of men and a variety of cases. Opening the door, I stand back and silently allow the entourage into my home. It's not lost on me that my place is about to become a temporary command post for whatever investigation she is working on. Without hesitation the men enter my home and busy themselves setting up computer and printing equipment as if it is the most natural thing to be doing.

Kerry walks into my kitchen and from the bag in her hand removes her supply of coffee as mine is not good enough for her. She blames her long hours. I blame her addiction to the black liquid. We agree to differ on this – she needs it to function.

"When was the last time you heard from Sam?"

Tension was building across my shoulders and in my mind. She had stormed into my home without warning and not even had the good manners to say 'hello'.

"Good evening, Kerry. I'm well thank you for asking. You're welcome to storm into my home and to take over with all your equipment. Please help yourself to anything you might need, be my guest!" I say, as I sweep my arm through the air in my kitchen. My outburst was an obvious shock to her, from the look on her face.

"Don't be so dramatic. I text you yesterday."

"If you did, I've not seen it."

"I've sent Sam on a mission but not heard from him once. When was the last time you heard from him?"

"Two days ago."

"Any news?"

"None he's shared. Kerry, he's probably taking a few days to rest. You do remember he's been stabbed?"

Kerry shoots me a look. She's not convinced that Sam hasn't shared any information with me. The truth is, if Sam is keeping things to himself he will have very good reason to be doing so and I trust him fully on that. He's the only person I can say that about. In all honesty, I don't actually know where he is right now. During our last conversation he was evasive and hadn't revealed his location – I'd no idea if he was still in Maldon or had moved on. For Sam to not have contacted Kerry could only mean one thing: he no longer trusted her. As much as I worried about his condition with regards to the stab wound there was one thing I could always rely on – Sam and I were the only people in this world who we could trust, and I knew he'd be onto something important and my contacting him could compromise that.

"I'm going to need to stay, if that's okay?" Kerry says, snapping me away from my thoughts.

"Not overly sure where you're going to sleep, if you plan on doing that. Follow me, there's something you need to see."

I walk towards my spare bedroom with Kerry hot on my heels. Despite her having sent Sam and I to the Collins scene she'd not received our reports yet. Set out before her is the story so far. She'd not seen this room either, with everything we know about Ashbeck mapped out in fine detail. She had her own copy of the files, but I knew she wouldn't have them available to view the way she is visualising them now.

The other side of the double bed, boxes are stacked against the wall. It's not lost on Kerry that they are still there. She helped me move in before Christmas, I'd taken the burden of Charlie's belongings for Sam because it had been too much for him to deal with at the time. He still hadn't faced up to that task.

"He's not dealt with it yet, then?"

"Bringing these here was the worst thing we could have done for Sam. He's hiding from reality, I believe."

"Hmmm," she says and turns back to the wall. "This is good work, Kate. I need coffee and to get the computers starting some searches."

Returning to my kitchen I was astonished to find the men had already left. The equipment was already set up and beginning to whir into action. The coffee filter machine had worked its magic and Kerry was now pouring it into two mugs that I'd handed to her. We hadn't seen each other for about a month and despite my initial annoyance at her unannounced arrival, we do get along.

Coffee in hand, she starts entering passwords and accessing the depths of information she has unlimited access too – there are several layers of protection that she has to pass, before she can start work. This takes time and, from memory, at least two coffees. Watching the scene unfold reminds me of when we first met and of watching Charlie and her daughter, Ruth working together in Kerry's kitchen in Norfolk. The memory, heavy on my heart, makes my eyes sting and I turn away. Mindful of my mood, she gives me a moment to compose myself. Kerry had become fond of Charlie in the short time she'd known him. He'd won her over with his 'you'd rather have me on the inside hacking out than on the outside hacking in approach'. His fingers had flown over the keyboard and his mind danced with ease around any blocks she may have tried to place on him. He'd also begun to date Ruth and they were inseparable: together they were a formidable team at pursuing the truth.

Startling me, my phone sounded from my inside pocket. The display, showing it to be JJ, I knew this call wouldn't be good news.

"Evening, JJ."

"Kate, I'm at a scene. You need to be here. I've called Sam and he's already on his way."

"Kerry is with me. She turned up thirty minutes ago."

"She'll want to see this too. Does Sam know she's about?"

"No, why do you ask?"

"I'll warn him!" He says, gives me the scene address and hangs up.

I let Kerry know.

"Any hint as to why we're needed at this one?"

"No. Its only about fifteen minutes away, so we'll soon know."

I drive because I know the roads and Kerry doesn't. My thoughts wander to the scene from earlier in the week and wonder if there would be children involved – I can't help but think about Jodie and wonder how she's doing. Deep down, I knew this would be connected to the Collins case and that Ashbeck was either killing again or pulling strings.

Kerry sat in silence while I spoke about the scene at the Collins house. I shared my opinions on the horrors of the scene – my thoughts that wouldn't see a report – she didn't react in any way. Her unresponsiveness unnerved me.

"The reports are almost done. We work on them when Sam calls me."

"There's no rush."

No rush? That is never the reaction from this woman. Something isn't adding up.

Arriving at the scene I spot JJ's car immediately and know he's been called in on his day off. He never comes to work in his sports car and I expect he was at the golf course. Parked beside him is Sam, leaning against the wing of his Mercedes speaking into his mobile phone.

My heart skips a beat and butterflies start to work their magic in my stomach – I can't help myself. Kerry must have caught me smiling because she rolls her eyes at me. As soon as the car comes to a stop, she jumps out and makes her way over to him. Without letting him finish his call, she starts her assault. I'm unable to hear what she's saying but am watching the conversation between them unfold before me an know I need to intervene – Kerry isn't holding back. If she's not careful she will get herself removed from the property. Sam, remaining calm for once, from what I could tell, wasn't responding which I know will be infuriating her. Heads were already turning in their direction and despite me not wishing to be involved I had already stepped out the car and was heading towards them.

"Kerry, Stop! Whatever the issue it needs to wait. This is most definitely not the time, or the place for you to be having this conversation. You either walk away or change the subject." I do not care that she's my boss, the woman is out of control.

"I've not finished with you, Sam!" Kerry shrieks, snatching my car keys from me. Within a minute she'd driven away.

Great.

"What was that all about?"

"I've been running a search and have established some facts. She doesn't like what I've found."

"She's set up one of her investigation command posts in my kitchen. These facts you've discovered, you need to share them with me."

"Yes. Not here though. Afterwards. Are you being serious, she's taken over your place?"

I nod, touch his arm and we start to walk towards the front door, towards JJ who is waiting for us.

"It's happening again, Kate." Sam says as we make our way towards the house. "I'm not sure we can trust our boss. Promise me you'll be careful."

"Can't I just come with you?"

"Not today. I need you to keep an eye on her, especially if she's at yours."

The sky is becoming stormy. JJ walks around the side of the

house and we follow. He's rubbing his balding head, which is something he does when he's stressed.

"There's no littl'un's at this one," he announces. "Thought you'd be pleased to know."

Sam inhales deeply and lets his breath out slowly. His shoulders relax slightly. Relief momentarily brushes with me, too. There are, however, bodies. Death awaits us, and I need to mentally prepare myself for it: never an easy task and if an outsider looked on they might think we were callous in how we respond to such sights. The truth is that without the dark humour that comes with the jobs we'd break within a few cases. It unites us.

"Right, just needed to show you this. See how the glass is broken in the same way as the other property? It looks like this ornament may have been used to break the glass, we're bagging it and taking it in."

Sam and I both nod, JJ isn't in the mood for hanging about and immediately turns and ushers us the way we've just come.

"Need to preserve the scene as the team haven't processed it yet, we'll go in through the front." He says as we head back along the side path, I'm leading the way.

"What are your initial thoughts, JJ?" Sam asks.

"Ah, my friend. I called you two here because I want my initial thoughts confirmed. I'm keeping it zipped. I need your input before I process anything."

"No pressure then!" I say, with a smirk as we come to the end of the path and walk side-by-side.

JJ's shoulders are showing signs of rounding, his hair has started to grey at the sides and there is a permanent furrow between his eyes from his constant frowning. Despite all these features adding a unique and charming appeal, I cannot help but be saddened that the stresses of his job physically show.

Turning to us JJ leans in,

"I wanted you both here for very good reason. Now keep your thoughts to yourself, ok. We'll talk about them in private. This case is connected for obvious reasons but there are differences," he taps his head, you'll see. "Come on, before that horrendous woman decides to come back."

He is, of course, speaking of Kerry. His first impression of our boss not a good one.

We walk through the house into the kitchen and the first thing I note is the gun on the table. It has been placed in an evidence bag and an officer is standing beside it.

"We left that in-situ, so you could see it. Thanks Jerry, you can take it away now, these guys will appreciate having visualised it."

Jerry nods his head at JJ, places the bagged gun inside a black case and seals it before carrying it away. Moments later Kerry walks in. JJ does not mention what she's just missed.

"I didn't realise you had started without me."

"Let's move towards the lounge. I have to warn you, it's a bit messy." He looks directly at Kerry in the hope that she shows a reaction. Truthfully, she has a stomach of iron. In the few months I've known and worked for her there hasn't been a single image or sight that she's reacted to. I doubted she'd start today.

The door to the lounge is open and the voices of those working the scene are audible as we approach. I recognise a couple of the technicians from the Collins shooting. JJ was right, this scene was messy – he talks us through what he has discovered so far, making sure to point out the ace of spades playing cards that have been torn in half and placed near the coffee table.

"These cards are the only aspect that connects these two latest cases to our original case. It's a flimsy connection at best." Kerry announces to the forensic team working the room.

Sam's anger spikes.

"So, on the whim of a flimsy connection you've felt the need to set up a command unit at Kate's place? Bollocks you think it's flimsy Kerry!"

Spinning on his heels, he walks away.

"Sam! I need to see you before you head off." I call after him, unsure if he's heard me or intendeds to take notice. I didn't want him leaving the city without saying goodbye. Especially when he was in a mood.

JJ needed to work his scene, which he preferred to do without police or private investigators poking about. There were enough police here already and I knew JJ would pass the information on, so I walked after Sam. Kerry headed to my car, where she sat and waited. She wouldn't like being made to wait. The stormy sky had turned to rain, the first drops were beginning to fall. Sitting in the front of his car watching as the droplets turned into a heavy downpour and streaked down the windscreen, both of us were automatically transferred to another time, into a memory from which neither of us could move forward. Reaching for his hand I squeeze it, giving unspoken reassurance.

"Why is she so angry at you?"

"Ha! I've run a search on her and she found out. I'm working on proving what I found out. I'm not sure you want to know."

"Do I need to know?"

"Yes, you do. At four years old Kerry was known as Kay Collins and she ran away from home at fourteen, leaving her younger sister behind. Guess where the family home was?"

I didn't have to guess. I knew. Sam wouldn't be sharing this with me unless he was sure.

"This explains her attitude towards you." I say, as my anxiety begins to surge.

"Sam, please don't make me go back with her."

Looking at me, with one raised eyebrow and through saddened eyes, he sighs.

"Just one night, Princess. I need one more night, then I'm coming to fetch you."

"Do you think Kerry killed her family?"

"No. I think she's covering for her sister. I just can't find her. I have no idea who she is. Not yet." Eyes remaining on me, he considers his next statement. "The only lead we have on that is the image we have from Jodie's description. That concept scares the shit out of me."

"Go home. Pretend you are pissed off with me and on her side. Fake tiredness at some point and have a bag packed by the morning. You and I are going away. I'll gather everything we need. Don't tell Kerry what we're up to."

"What do you think the torn ace of spade means?"

We'll brainstorm tomorrow, in the meantime I need you to get as much from grumpy drawers as you can. I need to know what our boss is up to."

"You know I love you."

"I love you too. Now go and I'll be over to get you in the morning. Be rested beautiful!"

He winks at me as I get out. Turning one corner of my lips into a slight smile, I slam the car door in mock anger. Sam fires the engine, and roars away. Storming over to my own car, opting for the passenger seat as Kerry obviously wants to demonstrate her power over me and is sitting behind the wheel.

Climbing in, I slam this door too – my mood beginning to feel convincing.

"I can't believe what he's done." Turning towards Kerry, I continue. "Are you aware of what he's done?"

"I have a fair idea, he used the laptop I gave him to do it. You're angry at him and not me?"

"What gives him the right to do that? He has blown any trust between you guys and I wouldn't blame you if you never trust me again. Sam and I have history. What the hell is he thinking?"

"Kate, I trust you! I've come to you for help! I've set up my equipment at yours because there is no one I trust more than you to help me do what I need." Kerry is looking at me and holds eye contact – her stare unblinking and stern.

"How do you want me to help? What exactly do you need?"

"I need to trace my sister."

"Okay, I'm sure we can do that. We should make a start as soon as we get back."

"It's not as easy as you might think." Turning her head away she starts the engine and drives away. "I need directions, its why I came back. I have absolutely no idea where we are."

Smiling to myself I give her directions as we chat.

"Did he tell you what he found out?"

"No," I lied. "I didn't give him the chance."

"You have a fire in you, lady." She chuckled.

"He's not confirmed it but suspects I'm the long-lost daughter of Will and Jane Collins." She confesses.

Wide-eyed, I turn towards her,

"Are you?"

"Yes, well not biologically but they bought me up. I ran away from home at fourteen, leaving my younger sister behind. That is my one true regret. Leaving her."

"Is that why you sent Sam and I to the scene?"

"Yes."

"And the fact that there was an ace of spades there, a complete coincidence."

"I'm not so sure on that."

Now home Kerry returns to her computer set-up while I made fresh coffee. Without much in the way of food in the house because of my intentions to move in with Sam, I opt for take-away. Removing the menus from the draw I place them on the table beside her.

"Not like you."

"No, I was moving in with Sam tonight, you've changed our plans somewhat. My fridge is empty."

"And the first thing he did was piss you off."

"I'll get over it."

"Finding my sister won't be easy. She doesn't exist. All I have is the registration number of her bike and the address of where she lives."

I shoot Kerry a look.

"How do you mean, she doesn't exist?"

"She's anonymous. Our true identities don't exist anymore. We were both removed from our biological family illegally a very long time ago. You already know who adopted us. Those papers are not legitimate. My sister chose not to become registered after she left their care. No doctors, she's never voted, and the list goes on. The company has used that to its advantage up until now. Now it seems she's played me for a fool."

"Your sister is part of us?" I'm astonished, "Have I met her?"

"Yes, you have. Sam has known her for years." Kerry looks up from her work and watches my face as realisation settles over me. "Jade," I say in a whisper. The facial resemblance now obvious: how hadn't either of us picked up on this before?

"So now you've made the connection you can help me trace her. She owns a popular bar in London so that's a good place to start."

"Where?"

"Covent Garden. It's hugely popular. I'd no idea how she afforded it until now."

Her fingers flew over her keyboard as I placed coffee beside her. Within a few moments a familiar image emerged. *Butterflies* was where Mel, Jen and I had met on the night of Ashbeck's escape and it now appeared on her screen: it had always been our favourite place to meet. I feel physically sick.

Further searches reveal that Jade wasn't the owner of the bar, that honour belongs to a company called Pyramid Establishments. Pyramid: we're back to symbolism. From one search it appears Jade is involved with Ashbeck – Kerry had already hinted that this is what she suspects and that she believes her sister killed their adoptive parents. The ace of spades at the scene gives us a link between the two also. The fact that the playing card is torn in half, the difference between the two murderers.

As the pieces begin to fit together, we continue our search. Having formed a list of other properties belonging to Pyramid Enterprises, Kerry passes some to me and I use the second computer to help. Like before, during the undercover operation last autumn, properties were in clusters spread over several counties. One, however, stood out to me: they owned some land in the New Forest. This was out of the ordinary and needed further investigation. Keeping my thoughts to myself I make a mental note to inform Sam.

Kerry concentrates on her sister's movements by entering the registration number of her bike into the system. With the amount of CCTV covering the United Kingdom these days, we'd be lucky to get a hit from this search, but it's worth a shot. If she's been issued with a parking or speeding fine, we may get lucky. While the computer continues its search, Kerry flicks through the menus and chooses pizza. Not my favourite but I'll go with it as long as it has plenty of kick to it. Dialing the number, she places the order, making sure to add extra jalapenos on one half. I give her a smile.

"Its arriving in half an hour," she says as the printer whirs into action.

20

BLOODY CONNECTIONS

True to his word, Sam arrives early to collect me. Kerry, still clicking away at her keyboard to trace her sister's movements is more civil towards him today. She shares with us the developments of her investigation, which is minimal. Producing his notebook from his pocket, Sam flips it open to reveal the image of Jade and slaps it on the table in front of Kerry.

"Jodie described the woman who shot her sister. I drew Jade."

"As soon as I heard, I knew," Kerry says. "I'd had suspicions for about a month and her computer access had been blocked since."

"Suspicions for what?" I enquire.

"She made a search that didn't sit right with me. Sam, the same one you made. Jade needed to know if there is a record linking her new name to her old one and our adoptive parents."

"Did she make the discovery?"

"No, she didn't." Stressed, Kerry runs her fingers through her hair and they remain there, holding onto her head. "That's something I blocked from her a long time ago."

"The fact I made that same search freaked you, Kerry."

"Yes, it did. I have no choice to take all of this to the Home Secretary. My career is over. This case will be compromised. It will appear I've been protecting my sister who I now believe to be working directly for Ashbeck. How twisted is that. You don't know the half of it."

Sam and I exchange glances – we're suddenly in a very difficult position.

"Why don't you explain the rest of it, Kerry?"

"I'll tell the full story at interview only."

Sam and I had intended to escape to his today but there's no way I'm leaving Kerry alone. I'd arranged for Jason to meet us here this evening and I was determined for her to be gone by then. Deciding to remain here, Sam and I set to work on the paperwork we'd fallen behind on. Reports needed completing and office time was limited these days. Just as we were settling, my mobile jumped into life. Reaching into my pocket, I retrieved it and looked at the display. I didn't recognise the area code.

"Kate Warwick," I say and listen as I feel the colour drain from my cheeks. "No, you must have the wrong number, I don't have a sister. What you're saying to me can't possibly be correct. I'm going to put you on speaker, so my colleague can hear you."

Sam gets up and shuts the door. The man, who'd identified himself as Alistair somebody from Aberdeen Police continues.

"Your DNA profile showed up on our database. Ms Warwick, because you work for the MET your DNA was stored for elimination purposes, correct?"

"Yes, I used to. Not any longer."

"My point is, when I ran this ladies' DNA through the system, we got a hit. It appears you are her only living relative. Listen, do you still have contacts. I could send the data to someone who understands it and they can explain it to you? This is legitimate."

"Yes, hang on."

After providing the work e-mail for JJ, I hang up. Sam is pacing. He pauses long enough to take my hand and give it a squeeze. Nauseous, I'm lost for words: how is it possible for me to have a sister and not know a thing about it? As I stare off into the distance, I'm aware that Sam is talking. Focussing on him, I realise he's phoned JJ. The two men, the only people I trust in this world, pulling together to help me. Leaving them to it, my mind drifts to what I've missed out on all these years: the love two sisters never knew and the grief that would leave me with.

Ending his call with JJ, Sam turns to me.

"Princess, you need to pack an overnight bag and your passport. Do you know where mine is?"

"Yes, it's in my safe."

"Stick mine in with yours! We need to get to Aberdeen. JJ is booking everything. Apparently, he still has all our details from the last time saved. We need to pop to mine so I can get some things together."

"Why do we need to go?"

Sitting beside me, burying his head into his hands and rubbing his face, he takes a moment. After what seems an eternity, Sam gives me his eyes.

"This case is linked to the Collins deaths. There is a DNA match suggesting his brother is involved or was at the scene at some point. I don't believe in coincidences and nor does JJ. You need answers and we need to check this out."

"We can't leave Kerry here."

"No, we will deal with that matter first."

Sam is back on the phone and soon through to Jason Redruth. I listen as he brings our meeting forward to this morning and requests he brings two officers with him: that there's been a development in the case that he needs to be a part of and it needs to happen as soon as he can arrive.

"He'll be here in half an hour. How you doin'?"

Shrugging my shoulders, I stand up and half smile. As I head towards the door, I turn my head.

"It's a lot to get my head around. I'll go and get some things together."

"I'll lock up and go and sit in the kitchen."

Just as I'm walking out my room, the buzzer to my door sounds. I open the building door without asking who it is, not wanting to alert Kerry who's about to join us. I open my door and wait for him to arrive.

Walking the three men through to the kitchen, I introduce Kerry to Jason. He introduces the other two men, Henry and Paul. I explain that there's been a development this morning that's resulted in Sam and I having to arrange a trip to Scotland, that JJ is arranging travel for us, so we could have our planned meeting, and sorry it's had to be bought forward. Kerry isn't convinced. The look of horror on her face is apparent. She shoots me a look that could kill.

"Kerry, I met with Jason last night, on our way home. He is here to view our wall, he's not seen our extensive few months of investigation and it's about time he did. Yes, we've shared what we know but there's something about visualising it the way Sam and I work. This case has been going stagnant and that needs to change."

"There's a trust issue in this case," Jason starts. "I've looked into the whole case and there's an incredible amount of corruption involved. I will get to the bottom of it."

"Kate and I have been through the case again this morning," Sam interrupts. "The new information that has been presented to us answers a few questions as to how and why the corruption has been possible. Kerry, its time you shared your full story with us all."

"Not here."

"Then I will share what Kate and I have found out. While Jodie, the five-year-old survivor at the Collins household was describing the woman who shot her sister, I did what I always do. I sketched her. The woman staring back was someone Kate and I know and have worked with. She is someone I have worked with a lot over the years. Jade. Kate and I have discovered that Jade and Kerry are sisters. We have also discovered that Kerry has known that Jade shot their adoptive parents since before we were involved in the case and that's why she wanted us involved. It was only coincidence that the playing cards were found. It's now apparent that Jade has been working for Kerry for a considerable time, on this case and also for Ashbeck. This case is truly compromised. Kerry claims to have suspected for a month." Sam was out with it, and we watched Kerry being arrested for perverting the course of justice.

Henry and Paul led Kerry away while Sam poured three coffees.

"Where does this leave our case?"

"To be honest, I have no idea. We'll need to speak to the Home Secretary, she answered to him. This case is a complex one and I know I'm not yet fully briefed on it. There seems to be information missing from my files."

"Yes, from ours too."

"Come, let's take a look and see what we have."

We enter my spare room and he is taken back by our work. The attention to detail presented chronologically with cards in place of the evidence that I know to be missing from the original case. I've spent hours searching my mind and going over each murder, each complaint, each link between victims. I've compared my memories to the evidence Sam and I were given before we went undercover and know that someone on the inside is covering for someone else. Could that be Jade? Did she have access to files?

"It took me a long time to notice, but the most staggering detail of all is the lack of faces from the original cases. While Sam and I were in Great Yarmouth last year, we met two of these women, they'd been relocated under the witness protection scheme. We believe the photographs of their faces have been removed to avoid us discovering their new locations. The two women who came forward were located opposite buildings Ashbeck owns. One of them opposite the building Mel Sage was being held captive in."

Allowing this information to penetrate, I sip at my coffee. Jason stands, with his hands on his hips studying the wall.

"What you've just said has astounded me. I knew something wasn't right with this case. You two obviously sense it too."

"Sense it? We've proven it!"

We continue to explain what we've been told by Aberdeen

Police this morning and share what Kerry had told us about Jade's movements: that her bike had been picked up by Automatic Number Plate Recognition (ANPR) cameras near to the location of the murder scene, after the event. She was involved at some level. Perhaps Ashbeck was, too. All he could do was stand and shake his head in disbelief.

"This is such a tangled web of intrigue, linked people and conspiracy. This runs far deeper than we have been prepared to consider. Every time you get close to an answer something happens to either one of you guys. Watch your backs!"

"What have you learnt from Interpol?"

"Right! It seems your hunch might be correct, Sam. There are unsolved murders dating back to the end of the Vietnam war, beginning as soon as US troops started arriving back home. Now, all the families that were attacked had someone out in 'Nam and they all belonged to the same platoon. Here's the thing, at the time the murders weren't linked as they were in different jurisdictions plus the military wanted it kept quiet as a lot went on during that war that was controversial. Families need closure and they pressed for answers, eventually Interpol became involved and linked the cases. We have a name. Alec Johnson. Mr Johnson arrived in England and we have a death record of his murder. What if the real Carl Ashbeck was murdered and his identity stolen?"

"Sam, as soon as you learnt about the ace of spades playing card that was your reaction. Your gut reaction is rarely wrong. Now we have this information to back it. I knew I was right to pursue this avenue at the time."

"We might have a body we can exhume. Ashbeck was given leave from prison to visit his sick mother. That's how he escaped. If she was buried, we can get DNA to confirm if she is his mother or not. Ashbeck's DNA is on record."

Nodding, Jason adds. "I've found out a little about Phil Andrews, I know you were all friends, so this may be difficult for you to hear." He waits for our reactions.

"He stopped being our friend when he crossed us and placed us in known danger," anger spikes Sam's voice.

"Fair enough. It appears he closed the investigation for his own gain. Families in America could have had the closure they needed years ago, and we have firm evidence collected from his property that confirms he helped Ashbeck escape from prison. Sam, that is partly thanks to your son and his dedicated work in surveillance. A talented lad."

Silence fell at the mention of Charlie, who had set up hidden cameras around Phil's house. He'd lived with him, his Godfather, at the time and had recorded his shady dealings with Ashbeck's gang members. He'd also managed to gain access to phone conversations, including one with Ashbeck himself the day of his escape. There were also boxes of the hoodies the gang wore stashed in Phil's office, purchase orders for goods and evidence of money received for them. In return for the favours Phil was giving, he was visiting Ashbeck in prison and gaining inside information on his life. On his computer was a manuscript.

Phil Andrews had been writing a book on murder. An insight into a psychopath from the perspective of one. Something for his retirement.

No wonder he'd pulled the trigger that day.

JJ had shown me the DNA match of the woman and confirmed she was my twin. He'd given me a hug and told me he was always about to talk if I needed him. Part of me wanted to pick up the phone and scream at my mother but what good would that do? I'd not spoken with her in years now, and it wouldn't change anything.

The three of us had spoken about the possible links of the Aberdeen case to our own. The facts emerging so far too complex to comprehend them being a coincidence.

The flight is full and leaves on time. Unable to talk freely in public, Sam and I have no choice but to remain quiet; giving me an opportunity to reflect. Unsure what I was expecting out of this trip or how I'm going to react at the sight of a dead sibling I didn't know existed was making me feel numb. There must be expectations of me from the investigation team and I'm sat here worrying I won't meet them: that this trip was about me walking into an investigation against me rather than anything else. Time would tell, I guess but the closer we got to landing the more anxious I was becoming.

When the seatbelt light pinged on, my hands started shaking which didn't go un-noticed by Sam. He held my hand as the plane lurched forwards and rocked to one side. Touch-down, bumpier than I'd prefer, not helping with my nerves. Taxiing to the terminal, I'm relieved when the plane came to a stand-still and I was able to stand up: claustrophobia was beginning to take hold of me and I needed air.

As soon as the plane doors open I'm out, leaving Sam to organise both sets of hand luggage. He's not far behind me and soon catches up. We walk through the tunnel leading us through the arrivals and into the main airport, which is tiny compared to the London ones. Both of us are astonished at the lack of passport control but I guess it's only an internal flight.

Without hanging about, we walk outside and the coldness of the air shocks me: I already know that I should have packed warmer clothes and am glad we're going home in a couple of days. Taxis are hanging about, and Sam walks towards them. Speaking to the first driver, he learns that he's been commissioned so walks along the line until he finds an available driver. We climb in and provide the address of the hotel.

According to the taxi driver we're in Dyce and Aberdeen is only ten minutes away. As we're being driven I take the time to look out the window. Our last visit to Scotland had been heart breaking because we'd lost Charlie, now I was heading towards the unknown. The buildings were doing nothing to cheer me up. As magnificent as their construction might be the dark grey stone used was mirroring my mood. Many were gothic in style: quite frankly, I needed cheering up.

Arriving outside the hotel, Sam paid in cash and we made our way inside. Needing to freshen up, I head straight for the shower. Its my way of washing the journey away. Sam, I know will disappear for a run. He always does. He'll return dripping wet with sweat and strip in the bedroom before plunging into a cold shower – which he was welcome to do alone.

Emerging from my hot shower, I wrap the warm towel around me and return to the bedroom. I'm not feeling at home here and need to get covered up. Drying with some haste and selecting clean clothes I cover my body, dry my hair with the hotel hair dryer and fill the tiny kettle with water. Sam won't be impressed with instant coffee, but he'll have a hot drink for when he returns. There's not much I can do confined to our room, but I busy myself until I hear the door click. Sweat glistens on his skin and soaks through his clothes. Stripping in front of me his clothing drops to the floor and he heads towards the bathroom.

"Did you enjoy your run, Pumpkin?"

"You've not called me that in ages and yes I did thanks."

His routine has gone a long way towards relaxing me – a sense of normality returning to our messed-up world, if only short-lived.

Deciding to curl up in bed, I lay there and wait for the sound and, as Sam gasps at the cold water, I let out a quiet giggle. Rather him than me!

I don't have to wait long before he's finished, and my eyes are met with the delight of his body. The towel doesn't hide much, and I can't keep my eyes from his toned body. Allowing it to fall to the floor, he slips beneath the covers and joins me. Sam's hands are soon gliding over my body as he snuggles up and pulls me close. His body, still cold from his shower presses against me causing goose-bumps and a shiver running the length of my body. With hardened nipples my body is responding to his touch as his hands make their way under my clothes. Removing my top, he begins nuzzling my neck as I wiggle out of my trousers. Now naked with our legs entwined and all thoughts of the day vanished, my hands begin to explore his magnificent body. My mouth finds flesh and I kiss the hollow just under his collarbone and gradually start moving up his neck towards his face. As our lips meet so do our eyes. Passion is immediate as the intensity between us grows and we kiss deeply as our fingers dance over skin leaving a trail of fire in their wake. Craving each other we can't hold back any longer. I need to feel alive. Sam rolls me onto my back and gently positions me, both of us let out a groan as he enters, and we make love, slowly.

21

REVELATIONS

Ashbeck had watched the strawberry blonde for weeks now and knew it was time. Finally, he was ready and knew Shadow was there to take control if needed – to step up if required. Everything had already been put into place for that to happen, he had been preparing her for this very moment.

Checking his watch, he noted that the woman next door would be coming out her front door and walking past his house in five minutes. For the first time, he intended to be outside to greet her: having lived there for some weeks now, he'd decided it was time they met. Stepping outside, he takes the few steps along the side of the house to unlock the cellar door and leaves it open before returning to the driveway. Making himself look busy he waits until she emerges.

"Ah! Afternoon. I'm Carl, been meaning to knock on your door to say hello," he calls out as he emerges from behind the hedge.

"Oh, hi Carl. I'm Cassie. I wasn't sure if anyone was about otherwise I've had said hello before."

Holding out his hand, Carl begins to walk towards her with

a broad smile on his face. Cassie walks towards him and to an uncertain future.

"It's really lovely to meet you, finally!" His enthusiasm is as strong as his handshake, which grips her hand and becomes slightly uncomfortable. Within a moment Cassie is restrained and in the cellar. With the door closed and locked behind them, any sound coming from her is muffled by his hand being firmly clasped over her mouth.

Within five minutes Cassie is face up on the bed with leather strops holding her wrists and ankles in place. Her mouth is taped closed, to stop her from screaming. Wide-eyed with fear, she looks on as Ashbeck busies himself with what he needs to do.

Walking over to his shrine he strikes a match and lights the candles, counting aloud as he goes about his routine,

"one, two, three, four, five, six, seven." Pausing to light a second match before continuing, "eight, nine, ten, eleven." Swishing the match through the air to extinguish it, he enjoys the smell of sulfur.

Turning to the series of bowls containing various necessities that he'd set up earlier, he washed his hands, dries them and places latex gloves on. Carrying a second, smaller bowl to the bed he wipes Cassie's left arm with a yellow liquid – from her chemistry lessons at school she knows its iodine, which this does nothing to ease her fear. Unwrapping a cannula, he takes a deep breath and inserts it into a vein in her arm. It produces blood, and he caps it. Success. He follows the same routine with her right arm too.

Using the iodine, he cleanses his own arm, unwraps a second cannula and inserts it into a vein. Again, a success which he repeats the other side. The tubes, already set up because he needed take his time with that process, are dangling above Cassie's head. Fetching a chair, he places it beside her. Connecting a tube to each of her cannulas and then to his, he begins opening the valves and starts the machine they are attached to. Blood starts flowing from each of their bodies, and he settles into the chair.

Wild-eyed, Cassie watches with horror as the scene unfolds before her – involved in some sort of rudimentary blood transfusion, if that's what it can be called.

She is going to die.

"If I remove the tape from your mouth are you going to scream?"

Cassie shakes her head, a tear escaping and rolling away as she does.

"You get one chance only, is that clear?"

She nods.

"You are a beautiful woman and I'm sorry it had to be you. Your sacrifice will save many others, so I hope that will count for something," he says as he removes the tape from her mouth with a gentleness she wasn't expecting.

"You will die too, you do know that don't you."

"I don't deserve to live because I've done many bad things. I need to die."

"Like this? Locked in a cellar swapping blood with a stranger?" Tears flow freely as she speaks, her voice shaky.

"I don't expect you to understand. I need your purity to cleanse me. I've done so many awful things. I can't die without being cleansed first."

"You're freaking me out."

"I expect I am. Trust me, you're having it easy, compared to the others."

"Others?"

"They've not made the connection yet, but I'm guilty of war crimes and have killed in America. I've killed over here which they caught me for, but I escaped from prison last year. I'm a wanted man. Do you remember that train crash last year?"

"Oh my God!"

"It is only a matter of time before I'm caught, and I've already been seen. I stabbed a man two days ago, he's hot on my heels again, I can feel it."

Feeling light-headed, Cassie closes her eyes and her body shudders as a sleepiness comes over her. Her body is feeling weak and she doesn't want to listen to his voice any more. A feeling of shame washes over her and she wants her ordeal to be over – trying to place her mind somewhere else and to block the sounds coming from him she wills herself to sleep and to slip away: for peace.

Yet his voice continues to drone on.

"I was very young when I killed for the first time. My young neighbour caught me doing something in the garden she'd ought not have. I just wanted to shut her up and certainly didn't mean to kill her, but I took it too far. That was the day I stepped up from killing animals to killing people. That was the day I found out that I preferred killing people, that I like to rape and mutilate. That I'm sick in the head. I could say that I hear voices, but I'd be lying. The simple truth is, it's what turns me on."

Metal crashes against splintering wood as the cellar door gives way. Men burst into the space, guns pointing through shields with raised voices as Ashbeck picks up the knife that lays beside him. His reactions, delayed by the situation he's placed himself in, compromise the power he thought he had today. This woman needs to die and now she may not. How could he be purified if she survives? He needs to take her life.

Now surrounded by armed officers, he can't see a way forward. Gripping the knife firmly, he takes the plunge towards her, but they are on him from behind, within a second.

Kate and Sam stand back letting the team do their work. Intelligence having led them to another cellar door. The last time they were in this situation, they'd saved Mel's life. It was, however a life half-lived now. Wondering what fate was in store for whoever Ashbeck had trapped inside this time, couldn't be helped – my mind raced with possibilities. Whatever it was wouldn't be good, that was guaranteed. They would have to live with the consequences of having met with such a monster, if they survived. Sam and I would have yet more images in our head of yet another crime scene of his making. Saying a silent prayer Ashbeck was inside this time, that we could finally return him to where he belonged.

Prison.

The cellar door gave way and armed officers entered, snapping my mind into real-time and forcing me to focus.

Shouting and commands came from below as they got the

situation under control, we were used to that.

"Jesus, fucking Christ! You need to see this!"

Looking at each other, Sam and I rushed towards the cellar, Sam got there first with me in hot pursuit. What greeted us took a while to process and comprehend – the damp and duly lit space taking us a few moments to adjust to. What met our eyes was such an inexplicable sight – briefly taking my attention from the fact that Ashbeck had been apprehended, finally.

"Katie-Ann Warwick, we meet again." He speaks boldly to me.

Sam steps between us, forever protective.

"Get me unattached from this freak! A woman screams from the bed.

Spinning around, Sam produces latex gloves from his back pocket and snaps them over his hands before placing pressure on her arm and sliding the first canula from her vein. Someone places pressure on the vein. He does the same with her other arm and the same person places pressure on that arm too. She is weak and I cannot help but wonder if their blood has mixed and her body has already started it's fight in rejecting his.

This man's capabilities never failed to sicken and astound me. Caught up in the glory of his discovery, he sits with a proud grin on his face that I'd like to swipe from him but I wouldn't give him the satisfaction of that.

"It's a shame I didn't get my time with you. I'd have enjoyed watching the life drain from your eyes, Katie-Ann." He is determined to continue with his torment of me.

"Warwick you need to remove yourself," someone from behind me announces. "I won't have you spoken to in this manner."

Looking directly at Ashbeck but directed at the officer in

charge, I speak with more confidence than I feel. My determination coming from the pit of my stomach, my reply is strong.

"I was his original arresting officer and I've been chasing him since he escaped, with P.I. Cooper. With due respect, I'm not walking away now. His words can't harm me. You have him cuffed and have unarmed him. He can't touch me. I will stay." I hold eye contact and refuse to look away from him. Locked in a battle of wills, neither of us willing to show weakness against the other.

Sam, having seen enough and knowing the truth of the damage this man has exacted upon my psyche, steps between us, breaking the deadlock. He knows how stubborn I am and would never ask me to leave the room at such a crucial point in the investigation. Yet he has my back just as I'd have his. The anger rising within me has me in a dangerous mood. Ashbeck has ruined so many lives, including people close to me. Intrusive thoughts enter my mind that I can't shake.

If Sam's gun was in my back pocket right now, I would probably use it.

I'm glad it's not.

Sam and I lead the way up the steps, Ashbeck follows cuffed, having had his rights read to him. He's held by two burly officers, who start walking him toward the awaiting car that will take him to the police station. He will be held there until transport can be arranged because he needs to be returned to prison. There will, of course be a whole series of paperwork and legal processes to go through, which all take time. The priority will be securing this man and ensuring he does not make it onto our streets again.

The walk isn't far but it's taking time. Ashbeck is moving forward slowly and the officers are allowing him that control.

There's a sudden roar of an engine as a motorbike approaches and navigates around the parked cars. My senses have been awakened and as her long hair and defined features come into focus I make a dash towards her. She's been brash enough to not wear a helmet – wanting us all to know who she is.

Ashbeck halts, a broad smile appearing on his face.

Raising a gun, she points it. Stopping in my tracks, Sam tackles me to the ground. She fires once. In a well-practiced movement her helmet is placed on her head and she's ridden away, a flurry of playing cards escape her hand like confetti as she departs. I didn't need to pick one up to know they'd all be identical – the ace of spades.

Her tribute to him.

Jade had just made her true association known to us.

22

OVER THE LINE

Stepping onto the street alone, without Chris, felt wonderful. Knowing, this time, he wouldn't follow empowering. One street away, waiting for Rachel's arrival, Greg Kingston sat in a secluded area.

Rachel had finally answered Jane's questions. Her eldest daughter was no longer in the dark about her father's past or under any allusions as to why he is missing. The man she idolised had crushed her heart and she'd had no choice but to leave her in pieces – at least Chris would take care of her while she headed off to oversee Max's rescue. Today had been too much for a young woman who'd been held hostage and had learnt that it was down to her father's need for satisfaction outside of marriage. Maisy, Rachel's younger daughter, had read their father's journal but was too young and therefore naive to comprehend its meaning and the severity of his crimes remain a blur to her.

Again, grateful that Chris had remained loyal to them, Rachel strode with purpose towards the van parked ahead of her and it suddenly dawned on her she may have overdressed.

Greg was probably the most brutal man Rachel had met. Short, stocky, robust. His mean looks appealing to her in a way she'd never understood before now. Captivated by the stories he'd shared with her at the kitchen table over the many cups of coffee together she'd become infatuated with this man – a man she'd never doubted had the capability to murder. She knew her marriage was in trouble and Greg had been emotionally unmoved by her advances. Now Max had vanished however, Greg was proving to be her most useful contact and perhaps her most trusted friend.

He'd always hated Max.

If her plan works out the pair would be formidable together.

Normally working alone, Greg insisted Rachel joined him. Determined she realised the depth of risk he was prepared to undertake for her. This exception, he hoped, would enable them to forge something special. A bond upon which they'd build a future. One of trust and respect: these elements were everything to him and everything to the operations he was willing to perform for her. He needed her on side. He needed her assurance.

What he truly needed was insurance.

Having her physically present was risky in itself but he was prepared to place a little trust in her. She was a strong woman who'd build a formidable reputation for herself in a harsh environment in a tough county. Essex wasn't known for flimsy dealings and she was among the toughest – a reputation she'd built almost overnight.

Nerves were, however, getting the better of her right now. Anticipating this he reached down beside him and fumbled for the flask he'd stashed beside his seat earlier, passing it to her.

"Here, drink this. It'll make you feel better."

"What is it?"

"Tea. It's sweet as."

Smiling, she opens it up and pours it into the small lid cup, takes a few sips and offers it to him.

"It's for you, babe. I've had all I need."

"Thanks, Hun."

Arriving ten kilometres out from their destination, he pulls over. Taking a bag from the back seat he presents Rachel with a bottle of water and a pack of sandwiches. She opens them. Taking one, he takes a delicate bite.

"Tuck in girl. You need to line your stomach and you need the strength."

She looks at him, her stomach churning with nerves. Putting one to her lips she takes the slightest of nibbles, obeying him in silence. Opening the bottle of water, she washes it down. They sit in silence, nibbling at food and passing the water between them. Smiling to himself when he drains the last of the bottle, he stashes it in the driver's door. Needing to keep it safe.

Continuing their journey, with the colour returned to Rachel's cheeks, he dishes out his instructions to her. Sitting, listening intently as he instructs her not to faint, not to look around for him, not to phone him. She'd be ready to take her husband's hand and join him by the ambulance once he'd been rescued. He'd be positioned ready for his role. If that opportunity didn't arise he follow them to the hospital and it would arise there. Deciding that might be the more viable option, depending on the volume of police presence.

Chris was under instruction to contact him if there was an emergency. That would give them legitimate reason to rendezvous after the event. He would collect the family and drive them to Rachel where he would take control of the situation.

Unsure how she felt about the prospect of seeing Max, Rachel was feeling uneasy. She wanted to be easily identifiable so was wearing her wig that best matched her public image from last year. Having walked with purpose towards the police station – having been dropped a safe distance from it – she could feel her hands shaking from nerves. The walk had only taken five minutes and she'd been grateful for the air and the opportunity to stretch her legs after the journey. The sense of being alone was usually welcome but it filled her with nerves this time.

Turning the corner, the police station was suddenly before her and she turned onto the pathway. Walking inside and up to the reception desk she introduced herself, signed in and was escorted within the depths of the building to be briefed. Security was tighter than she'd anticipated. Listening intently, she desperately wanted to relay a message to Greg but didn't dare. He'd make a professional judgement, she just had to trust and have faith in him.

Time ticked slowly while she waited for action, anxiety rising as thoughts of all that could go wrong formulated in her mind. Deciding the half hour journey from here to the final destination would be the worst part, she willed it to be over.

Eventually, a call to action was announced and she was bundled into an unmarked car. They held back allowing those involved in the raid to proceed first. Frustration bubbled within her as her heart pumped and the people who were keeping her company asked too many questions. Mindful to keep her mouth closed and her thoughts to herself she resumed her vow of silence. They didn't make it easy though. Constantly hounding her with information she wanted was followed by a question she was expected to answer.

When they finally arrived all hell had broken out. Screens shielded the ambulance and Rachel's car was met. An officer stepped out to have a quiet word, before returning to the car.

"No questions. We need to turn around and head back." He said.

"But, Max, please. Please let me see my husband!" She hoped her performance sounded convincing.

"We need to get you out of here," was all he was prepared to say.

Inwardly, Rachel was smiling and hoped this didn't show to her travel companions. It felt good to be a widow.

23

ROAD TRIP

Ashbeck had signed control of all his business assets to Shadow two days ago. Moving quickly to protect her interests she'd given power of attorney to her niece: who she believes to be her daughter – she'd always felt a special bond towards the girl and the diary she discovered in the safe at her adoptive parent's house had certainly added to those feelings. Everything she'd ever felt, now slotting together and making sense.

Revealing her identity to Kate and Sam had been a bold move. It would have been just as easy to have assassinated Ashbeck wearing her helmet, but she wanted them to know who was in the game now: just how compromised their precious case was. She could ride away smiling knowing how much more truth there was to uncover, and how Kate's world would one day be blown apart – if she survives that long.

Needing to get away again, and not knowing how long she'd be this time, there was some business to attend to first. Ashbeck had handed her three of his best operatives six months ago and their loyalty to her was about to be tested now he was gone. It was time to flex her muscle in the cruel world she now inhibited alone. She'd hung on his every word during her training and, as she sat in her bar waiting for their arrival, sipped at neat vodka contemplating.

One prisoner she'd very much like at her disposal, who'd been missing from the public eye for a few months now, was Max Smith. The once deputy commissioner was several miles away from the city. She'd had thoughts in her mind to take a trip that would finish him off, but someone had beaten her to it.

Her business of being a double agent put her in a good position to know where important people were and any given point. The arrangements she was now making were more important than him. Two missions were on her list for her personal attention. Locating Rachel Smith had become one of her main priorities. She was causing trouble and making quite the name for herself. The agent she'd sent undercover to locate her, despite the tracking system she'd placed upon him, had gone off grid: rather he'd located it and had abandoned it as it hadn't moved for three days. That, or he was dead. She had lost control of the situation and panic was setting in.

Glancing at her watch, she noted they'd only got thirty seconds before they were late. Just as she was beginning to consider what their punishment might be they burst through the bar doors and made their way towards her.

Knocking back her vodka in one mouthful, she silently makes her way through to the rear of the property.

"Follow me."

Abiding, they follow her into a corridor running the length of the bar with varying doors leading from it. Shadow walks with purpose towards the far end, keys jingling from her left hand. Stopping at the door, she unlocks it and pushes the door inwards. Standing aside, she beckons the men inside.

"There are three in there. I need them gone without any trace. I've been assured you're the best."

"We won't work for you, love," the taller one of the two states. Removing her gun from her inside pocket, taking aim and firing a single shot takes a split second and she hits him in the middle of the forehead. Holding eye contact with the second man, she has a simple question:

"Do you work for me?

"Yes, ma'am. I'll have a replacement here and this lot cleared up within two hours."

She'd made an impact, stated her claim on the gang. They would conform or get shot. Her respect had been earned tonight. Fear ruled in the hierarchy again tonight.

True to his word, the four bodies had been removed and any trace of them cleaned away. They would be rewarded on her return.

Needing to disappear and having left her precious bar in the safe hands of three trusted gang members, Maldon was a memory. Ashbeck forever etched deep within her psyche, Shadow was heading towards Scotland again. Now past Edinburgh, she'd enjoyed the A68 from Darlington. It had given her something to concentrate on other than monotonous motorway riding. Cambers, accents and descents – the thrill of riding her bike.

Her uncle was being careless, so her intervention was required. Finding the perfect property had been simple and the keys were ready for collection and the main reason for her trip. She needed to see her aunt too for she has a special task for her. Hopefully it will get her on side, but it was a risk to let this fragile minded woman into the darkness that hung over the family she'd married into. They'd always been close, and right now she needed a confidant.

Arriving after dark, completely unexpected she parks her bike and pounds on the front door ready to place her shoulder against the wooden structure and her foot over the thresh-hold: as soon as it opens a crack, she makes her confident entrance.

Without any doubt her aunt and uncle are shocked to see her. Fear of their safety as thoughts of his brother and sister-in-law (her parents) and of their own morality seep into reality for them.

Smirking at the shocked look on their faces, Shadow strides through the house into kitchen without removing her boots, knowing this would annoy her aunt. Removing her gun from her inside pocket, she places it on the kitchen table that now acts as a barrier between them. They'd followed a few paces behind and, by the looks on their faces, are taken back by the sight. With each breath, a new wave of fear shudders through their bodies.

Filling the kettle before lifting herself onto the worktop to wait for it to boil, she reached inside her jacket. Both relatives flinch as their anticipation becomes too much to handle. They relax slightly when she removes a document from her pocket and throws it onto the table.

"A gift for you both," the first words are finally spoken. "Take a look, its perfect."

Edging towards the table he lifts the paper and unfolds it. Retreating he shares the images with his wife.

"Why?"

"You need it, do you not?"

"But we're happy here," her words are unconvincing.

"You've outgrown this place now." Looking at her aunt, and then her uncle, "pour a large brandy each, I'm not sure tea will be strong enough."

"You 'aving one?"

"Only if I can stay."

Without an answer he walks away, returning with three glasses with generous measures of golden liquid inside.

She has his attention.

Standing in the kitchen, they sipped at brandy. A silence had fallen between them that Shadow allowed; she wanted the alcohol the take effect, so they relaxed a little.

Taking her aunt by the hand, she then led her towards the lounge. Sitting side by side on the sofa, she took both her hands into hers and gave them a gentle squeeze. Considering her words carefully because she's under no illusions that this gentle woman has no idea of the type of family she has married into, she begins to share with her the details of the family business she now jointly owns with her husband.

There was no reaction, and this surprised Shadow. Looking her aunt directly in the eyes she waited for a response from her.

"Your mother shared what was happening with me a very long time ago. She wanted you to come and live with us and it was all planned, but you chose to live with your sister. She'd made a good life for herself and your uncle and I thought you'd be better off with someone younger."

"I wish I'd have been given the choice."

"Yes, knowing what I know now, so do I pet."

Swallowing hard, Shadow places her emotions away: she has

become too good at that.

"How much do you know about the business?"

"I know about the adoption scheme and how that works. That's how they ended up with you girls, did you know that?"

"Yeah, we found that out a long time ago."

"How about what's in the cellar?"

"The cellar?"

"Oh, you only know a small portion of what's been going on." Leaning her head back and closing her eyes, Shadow takes a deep breath and sighs. "I'm so sorry but you need to know what you're involved in."

"Can't I just walk away, get myself a little cottage and have you visit me from time to time, when you need to escape?"

"You'd let me do that?"

"You're here now and I'm certain that you're the one that killed them!" She holds Shadows gaze, "yes, I was a little startled that you turned up at first because I didn't expect you to, but it is lovely to see you and you are welcome here, always."

"You don't know how much that means."

"Oh, I think I do, love. Now, I also think you need to tell me what my stupid husband has got mixed up in during this past week because he's in a right panic. He thinks I'm stupid and that I don't listen to the news! Did he murder that woman in his hut?" She was out with it.

"Yes, and he has messed up. Don't panic though, hopefully I have covered for him. Before I took my revenge back home, I made some changes to stored data. My sister had blocked me from some of it, but she seems to have forgotten that you two exist. As far as the authorities are concerned, you two are non-existent. This house was owned by my father and all of his property is now owned by me. Your name is associated to this dwelling, so I have purchased a new one in my company's name, and you need to move into it. It's not far away, so you'll get to keep all your friends."

"What did he do to her and why?"

"The family business isn't just about adoption. There's another side to it. He used to get orders for body parts from collectors and he's left his businesses to you two. The people involved won't take no for an answer. I'm here to help you cope with how to deal with that."

"My Matt killed that woman for a body part?"

"Yes."

"What did he take?"

"Her face."

"Was she still alive?"

"I've not seen the police report yet." Shadow lied.

24

PROTECTION

Greg Kingston jumped into action. Chris had phoned him, as he'd been instructed to. He now had legitimate reason to be involved. He'd shared that Rachel was already tied up answering questions and she'd requested the family turn up tomorrow. Apparently, Jane needed time to organise what she and her siblings would need.

He'd already booked rooms at a pub close to where Rachel was. She would be joining them there too. A short text to Chris confirming the arrangements had been sent.

Plans were falling into place, making him feel good about himself. Arriving back at his private residence, he parks his vehicle and enters his property. Retreating to the lower level via his spiral staircase he descends into the depths of his sterile domain. This is no ordinary space. Entering the first room he passes the chair that's bolted to the floor in the centre of the room. The leather straps attached to it, dangle freely for now. The flooring, the dark grey of Welsh slate, a harsh contrast to the white-wash walls. You enter this place under duress to die: there's no torture, no chances to change his mind, to defend your honour. This was a place that required washing down whenever used. Assisting with that, the pressure washer sat in the far corner always ready for action, right now it covered the drain that soaked directly into the ground.

Disposal was easy. His bodies were taken out to sea, not one of them had ever been found.

Diagonally opposite the pressure washer was a door leading to a smaller room and this was the space he required now. Opening this door, he entered and removed the water bottle from the bag he was carrying. Until she'd earned his trust Rachel Smith's DNA, combined with his own, would sit in his own evidence bank and would act as his personal insurance policy. Sealing it into a bag, he wrote the date, names and the time-stamp from his CCTV on the label and placed into his safe and hoped this would be sufficient.

Falling into family-friendly mode he ventured up the spiral staircase to his living quarters, where he made a cuppa. Taking it to his lounge, he dials Chris's number again to confirm arrangements with him for the morning. He'll be collecting the family at six. He hoped Jane could have the baby ready by then, and that it wouldn't cry all the way to the New Forest. They'd arrive together, solidarity in their support for the grieving widow.

How he wished he could share her bed already.

25

ABANDONED

Stepping onto the platform, my heart rate quickens: anxiety still an automatic response in railway stations since the knife attack. Sam, having promised to meet me, is nowhere to be seen which isn't helping matters.

Rushing towards the exit and fumbling in my handbag for my phone, I curse under my breath that it's become buried in the depths of what I insist on carrying around with me. Finding it eventually, I'm dialing Sam's number as I walk onto the street towards the taxi rank. Unusually distracted, I'm not paying attention to my surroundings and don't notice the white van until three men have descended upon me and are bundling me inside of it. One of them snatches my phone and throws it out the door before it slams shut, casting darkness over the space. My whole body, trembling with fear is thrown onto the cold floor as the van lurches forward into the traffic. Twisting our way through the streets of London, my body restrained from behind, I'm unable to fight back as my ankles are bound. Blinking a few times allows my eyes to adjust to the poor light and I can make out some features of the two men in front of me. Frozen with fear as one of them grabs an arm and forces it towards him – looping a cable tie around my wrist he secures it. The man behind me lifts me to free my other arm, which is forced towards the other. The man's face, just inches from mine, is illuminated by the light from the windscreen, his chiseled features familiar. I'm suddenly taken back to my underground car park and to the night I was assaulted – to my blouse being ripped open and the ace of spades playing card that was placed inside my bra.

Suddenly I know I'm in deep trouble – I'd watched him being arrested and can't believe he's been released.

Once my arms are secure, he backs off and the second man comes into view. Taking in his shaven head and the darkness of his eyes, I follow the shape of his nose and the thin line of his lips that curl up into a sneer. He has a mean, angry look about him that I commit to memory.

Restricted by my restraints, I try to look at the third man but he's still behind me. I catch a glimpse of blonde hair that's tied back. He's forcing me to lean against him, holding me firmly but not hurting me. I was sensing something different about him. The other two had backed off and settled against the side of the van, to a place I couldn't see their faces which is fine by me. Suddenly feeling a heaviness coming over me I'm struggling to stay alert. His grip around my body all I can focus on as I drift into the unknown.

Slowly becoming aware of sound, of tyres rolling on tarmac, it takes me a few moments to remember. Panicked, I fight against my restraints. The sudden movements cause nausea to engulf me: acid burns the back of my throat and I'm turned onto my side as I gag and fight the need to vomit. Tears burn my eyes as I swallow hard a few times.

Allowing me to sit up, the man behind me opens a bottle of water and offers it to me.

"Slow sips," he says as he holds the bottle to my lips. As the water hits my stomach it causes another bout of gagging sensations. Believing I've been drugged – my legs and arms feel numb and my head foggy – I raise my knees and rest my head upon them. Taking deep breaths. I allow the feeling to subside.

"It's because you moved quickly. You'll be fine. You need to lay back down."

Doing as I was told, he helped me. His eyes caught in the light from the windscreen, their piercing blue colour catching me off guard. Emitting a kindness that didn't fit in this situation: this man was beautiful – captivating, almost. The other two are harsh and cruel looking but this one is not. With a soft and gentle look about him, an intensity that is intriguing and spellbinding. His face was committed to my memory too.

Remaining focused and un-phased was becoming difficult as it dawns on me that they've allowed me to see their faces and the danger this has placed me in. Trying to move my hands and legs to gain some comfort I become frustrated. The blonde man holds my shoulders and eye contact. He simply shakes his head and I know to be still.

Beginning to tremble again, my body is showing outward signs of my predicament as it dawns upon me that I'm kidnapped and that, perhaps, Sam has been too. He hadn't shown up at the station when he'd promised to: oh God, what if he was already dead?

Fear enveloped my existence as Jade entered my mind. How long would it be until she and I were face to face with her pointing a gun at my head? Images of Sam start dancing in my mind: he has bullet wounds all over his body and Jade makes me look at them. In another image, she forces me to watch as she shoots him. My sobbing becomes uncontrollable: and then there is darkness.

Detecting movement again, I shift my head in time to see the blonde man is pulling a mask over his head. He taps his left cheek and I focus on a star below his eye, convinced he's just winked at me from behind his mask, I look around me. The other two men also wear masks now. One has a teardrop and the other a moon.

Remember the star. Remember the star. I chant inside my head as I realise all concept of time has escaped me and I've no idea how long the journey has been. Feeling groggy again, I knew I needed to remain still for a while after the last nauseous attack. Unable to focus, my muscles uncooperative, my head fuzzy and with my vision dipping in and out I bide my time before I move.

Still travelling, without the stop/start motion of the city the continuous drone of tyres on tarmac is hypnotic. Vibrations shuddering through my body are making my eyes roll upwards as I fight to remain awake. Sam continues to occupy my thoughts: visions of his demise evoke a fear too grave for me to comprehend. Anxiety, now out of control turns into panic and I begin to fight for breath.

A sudden change in tyre tone and terrain awakens my senses, bringing with it a new wave of adrenaline and a focus on my breathing: bumping at speed along a track, I'm being bounced around on the van floor. Steeling a glance through the front window, skywards, to try and establish a sense of location. Trees surround me. We slow slightly, as the track becomes rougher and the canopy overhead thickens. Time seems to stand still as seconds last forever, making my journey into hell linger. Wishing it possible to close my eyes and give in right now, because that seems a viable option, as the uncertainty of my fate is too much of a burden.

Turning sharply and coming to an abrupt halt, two of the men leap out, leaving the man with the star on his mask with me. Glancing over his shoulder, he watches as the driver and the other two vanish from sight.

"You need to stop making eye contact with me, lady. They see that, and they'll force me into unthinkable things. Do you understand?"

Looking away, I nod. A tear slipping down my cheek, that he gently wipes away.

"Stay strong. I'm going to make your transfer look mean so help me with that and it won't hurt, okay. Don't make me hurt you. Fight a little if you want because they are expecting that of you."

"What do they want with me?"

"Information."

"Tell Jade from me to go to Hell."

"Hmmm, you think I'm telling her that?"

"You're scared of Jade?"

"We don't get to call her by her name. How do you know this is her?"

"What do you call her?"

"If I tell you that, I'll have to kill you."

"I'm going to die anyway. So, you may as well tell me."

"You have courage, I respect that. Shadow."

"What do I call you?"

"Good try."

"I'll think of something."

"Quiet now."

Seconds drag as the silence hangs between us in the air in the back of this rancid space. The sound of a fist bashing on the rear door startled me, and I jump. With a soaring heart-beat, I once again feel adrenaline pump through my body, every part of me wishing I could flee but knowing my ankles were tied together. With fear in my eyes I take one last look at the man before me and see a kindness in his eyes behind the mask, but it does nothing to settle me.

"I'm going to move you soon. To do that you need to walk. Don't attempt to run. They will have tasers aimed and you'll be on the ground in seconds. Do you understand?"

I nod.

From his back pocket he produces a knife and slices through the bind, throwing it to one side. My limbs are stiff from being in one position and from being on the van floor. He helps me to shuffle towards the doorway and I swing my legs, so they dangle towards the ground. As soon as they hit the dried mud track the temptation to run is overwhelming: a hand takes hold of my arm and grips it firmly – I'm not going anywhere.

They've parked in a clearing: evergreen trees encircle us, reaching skyward. I couldn't see any buildings. Visions of

Charlie's crime scene emerge, of his body tied to a tree and of his gunshot wounds. Was this their plan for me? With trembling legs, I'm asked to stand and forcibly encouraged to walk.

"You'll feel wobbly to start but I'm here to support you if you need it. You need to walk to the front of the van."

With slow, steady steps I conform because I have no choice. Three men watch with their tasers in clear view. Grimacing expressions adorn their faces. My stride is weak and unsteady, and I'm forced to lean against the man who pretends to be kind to me – it's not something I'm comfortable with but what choice do I have? In the midst of my anguish, I'm grateful for the warmth of his body as it penetrates my clothes, warming my cold and aching muscles. He's holding me so close that I can feel his warm breath in my right ear, sending shudders through my body.

"Keep it together," he says.

When we get to the front of the van I'm led to an opening in the ground: A trapdoor which has been propped open by a broom handle. Steps descend under the forest floor to uncertain horrors that await me. An old case flashes through my mind from cases that I read about: nothing positive.

Attempting to stand my ground, I try and refuse to take the first step into hell. His arm slipped to the small of my back and with an encouraging shove, I took my first tentative step down to stop myself from falling.

One, by one I descend the thirteen steps into darkness.

Thirteen.

From researching into Illuminati symbols with Sam, I know Ashbeck's legacy lives on.

26

THIRTEEN STEPS UNDER

Darkness invades the underground space in which I'm being held. The tiny room in which I'm held smells of earth and contains a rudimentary bed, a bucket and a bowl of water. With just the clothes on my back and a blanket they've given me, I'm freezing cold. The water I have left, I'm saving for drinking. Last night hadn't provided a positive outcome for food. Hunger deprivation the first tactic they were targeting me with. Candle light flickered in the corner, for which I was becoming thankful: the only light-source and warmth in this squalid place.

    Keys jingle in the distance and I cock my head to one side attempting to listen: footsteps grow louder as my heart, once again, beats faster within my chest. They stop outside, and I hear a key against the metal of the lock on my barred door. As it turns, the door swings inwards and someone walks in. Remembering his words, I don't make eye-contact with the man who'd shown a little compassion yesterday. Instead, I withdraw to the furthest corner and sit on my bed with my knees hugged against my chest and my chin resting upon them. Behind me, my blanket rests, neatly folded because I refuse to not have pride despite my dire situation.

Moving towards me, with a calmness about him, he sits beside me. Reaching over, I flinch but he doesn't touch me. Instead, he unfolds my blanket and places something there before folding it back over.

"Save that for later," he whispers "you'll need it. Don't let anyone see you with it."

Having no idea what he's given me I hope that it's food.

"Thanks."

"How you doing today?"

"What've they got in store for me?"

"I'm not sure. They might ask me to do stuff. I'll have no choice. You understand that, don't you? I have to follow orders." He looks at me, "look at me."

"You told me not to."

"It's just us here now."

Slowly, without moving my head I allow my eyes to drift towards him. His features memorising in the candle light, the flame reflecting in his bright eyes. I feel a warmth run through my body and am immediately disgusted with myself.

"Today will be tough, Katie-Ann but you will survive. Whatever they have planned for you my orders are to make certain you go hungry tonight. They want you to live. Now, you do well today, and I'll see what I can find for you on the food front later."

My heart sinks a little – whatever he's placed inside the blanket isn't food.

Glancing at his watch, he looks up at me.

"I hate this, understand that. I need for you to remove your clothes. All of them. They need you naked for this."

Startled and wide eyed, I look anywhere but at him. Nervousness overwhelming me at the thought of removing my clothes and the vulnerability of having him see me like that.

"You do know what they are going to do to me."

Despite the dim light I knew from his reaction. The look in his eyes, despite it lasting a split second, told me he knew what I would be enduring today, but I could also see compassion.

"Hand me your clothes and I'll fold them for you. We need to get moving. They want you ready by the time they arrive."

With shaking hands, I slip my shoes off and place them under the bed. Item by item, I remove my clothing as tears flow freely down my face. He reaches for me to wipe them away, making me flinch. His touch, warm and gentle against skin, and confusing my fragile mind.

"If they make me do anything, please know I don't mean it." He says as he moves closer to me, his hand still resting on my cheek, and our faces now just inches apart.

My body, on high alert, trembles with coldness mixed with nerves and when his hand travels from my cheek and his fingers trace the contours of my neck and travel towards my breast I shudder.

"We need to go. Can I trust you to walk with me or do I need to bind you?"

"Please don't make me go anywhere."

"There's no choice, Princess."

Princess. How does he know what Sam calls me?

Taking my hand, he gets me to stand and makes me walk out through the door. The darkness of my room is soon replaced with an illuminated, but narrow tunnel. Wrapping my free arm around my body, as some sort of protection I am dragged along. No words can describe what's going on inside my head, the fear and anticipation that I feel for the unknown horrors that await me. I can see a gun in his pocket, I know I have to conform if there is any chance of survival. I also know that if the opportunity arises I will have that gun out of his pocket.

Time seems to have a habit of standing still in my mind these days, and this tunnel seems endless. At the far end is a bright light, giving the illusion of walking towards death. It's not lost on me how this is supposed to make me feel but I'm stronger than that. Very clever, but Jade will have to try harder to break me even when I'm naked. From somewhere deep within I find some reserve: an inner strength kicks in.

Surreal as it is, walking into the light ends the journey. A door opens, and two men greet us. My escort is dismissed, and they take over. I'm led inside a room. The spotlights are vivid and the hum of a generator somewhere in the distance a constant noise in my ears. Glancing about me to gauge my new surroundings there's not much to see. A wooden structure is central to the small room, It's higher at one end than the other. If I was to guess the angle, I'd reckon a gradient of twenty degrees – innocent looking if it wasn't for the four cuffs attached.

The two men hadn't spoken to me. One had hold of each arm while I stood between them, my nakedness on show and my body refusing to give up trembling. In a flash of movement, two more men appeared, and I was being handled: fear engulfing me as I was turned upside down and fastened onto the wooden structure, head pointing downwards and feet towards the ceiling. Blood rushed into my head. Each man securing a limb each, I was unable to move far. I could turn my head, and that was about it. My heart felt like it was beating its way through my chest – I wish it would just give up.

Water dripped onto my face, making me jump. Struggling

against the cuffs binding me to the wooden structure my body rigid, I screamed. Water fell faster.

Suddenly there was water dripping on my face. However much I turned my head, there was no getting away from it. Fighting against my restraints, my whole body in panic, I couldn't catch any air as I tried to breathe. Water ran into my mouth and up my nose making me cough, breathing more water than air. Relentlessly, the onslaught of water continues as these people attempt to kill me.

I'm going to drown.

Water stops dripping but it does nothing to ease the rate of my heart. Taking hungry gasps of air, I choke as a wet cloth is lodged into my mouth: the water from it trickling down the back of my throat. Bile rises from my stomach, burns my throat and fills my mouth. Every cell in my body fights to not inhale. They remove the cloth and I spit the substance out. One of the men empties a bucket of cold water over my face, washing the vile liquid away, sending me into another panic.

"Where is Rachel Smith?" One of them screams at me.

Unable to answer that, I'm instantly aware this will be a long day. I shake my head.

"I don't know." I gasp.

The dripping re-starts as I begin to face the ordeal again. Focusing I attempt to empty my mind. All I'm aware of is the sound of the water echoing constantly inside my head.

Losing count of how many times they put me through this

and how many times they question me, my body eventually gives up its fight. No longer can I strain against the cuffs that restrain me. Coldness has seeped into the depths of my bones and I can hardly move. The water ceases, and he returns with a blanket and we are left alone. In silence he unclips the cuffs and helps me to sit. Blood drains from my head and a dizziness comes over me. Once that passes he helps me to my feet and wraps the blanket around my shoulders. I gather it around me, grateful to be covered and for the small amount of warmth it provides.

With his arm around me and my body leaning against his we take the long, slow walk towards my gloomy room: my sanctuary in this madness. Walking a million steps from this place could never remove the memory of it but I wanted to walk them. I needed to walk them: to remove myself away from this place and the sound of dripping water that will forever be imprinted on my psyche. Placing one foot in front of the other becomes easier as my muscles warm.

Once back inside the room, he leads me to my bed and I'm grateful to sit. No words have exchanged between us. I'm numb with cold, exhausted and so incredibly hungry. Unfolding my blanket he removes his gift to me, a foil blanket, and he gently unravels it. Placing it around my shoulders, before placing my own blanket over everything.

"Give me a little time and I'll return with some food and a hot drink. They won't hang about. Get yourself warmed up, okay."

Unable to respond, I sat huddled as far away from him as I could, my whole body shivering with cold. I didn't look up as he walked away and locked me inside the room.

Arriving with food and a new candle, he's smiling at me. I'd been sat in the dark, my candle having expired. Remaining in the same position that he'd left me in I'd cried until there was nothing left of me to give. With trembling hands, my attempt at holding a fork was futile.

"Okay, I'm going to help you. You need to eat. Let's get you spun around so we can do this."

Placing the food on my table, next to the candle, he turns his attention to me. He helps me to turn myself around so that he can sit beside me. Still naked beneath the blankets I'm unwilling to let them go and my hands clasp as tightly as possible. He notices the clothes behind me.

"Come on, let's get your clothes back on quickly. You'll feel more comfortable."

Picking them up, he pushes my top over my head and helps me with my arms and does the same with my jumper. My muscles are so stiff from cold that I struggle. Blushing as he helps with my knickers, but grateful that he's looked away I start to feel slightly at ease.

"Okay, wrap one blanket around your legs and the other around your body and let's eat before it gets cold."

Still unable to hold the fork, he alternates between taking a mouthful himself and letting me have food. Eventually conversation starts to flow from him and he shares a few things about himself. Captivated by his beauty and his kindness I listen as he pours hot chocolate from a flask into two mugs. Placing mine into my hands I wrap my fingers around the mug and am grateful for the warmth it provides. His hands encase my own, as he guides it to my lips and I take a sip. Settling back down beside me, closer than before, he lifts his arm and invites me to lean against him. Unsure why, I feel compelled to do so and a comforted feeling comes over me.

27

BETRAYAL

Waking to the sound of an alarm, it takes me a few seconds to realise the nightmare I find myself in: the candle in the corner of the room the first reminder and the smell of dirt the second. Warmth has returned to my muscles. Feeling movement behind me, I freeze and take a moment to assess my situation again. An arm rests over me, a hand under my clothing, against my stomach. Feeling the warmth of breath on the back of my neck does nothing to calm me. Trying to move away, the grip around me tightens and he pushes himself against my back, one knee pressing into the back of mine and the other leg moving over to hold my legs down. Unable to move my body, I try to free myself with my hands.

Panic is setting in and my fight begins.

"Hey, hey! Stop! I'm not going to hurt you. Just keeping you warm." He says, as he releases me. "You were so cold, you huddled into me, do you remember that? We both fell asleep."

"You can't blame a sleeping man for wandering hands. I'm sorry. Now settle back down, you need to rest."

Rest. Like that was going to happen.

Feeling tense, I obey. What choice do I have? Laying down as far away from him as I possibly can in the small space that we now seem to share. His hand, behaving long enough for me to close my eyes, finds my body and he gives out a contented sigh as he meets flesh once more. Recoiling again, I bring my knees towards my chest and begin to cry.

He holds me firmly but tenderly and, gradually my tears stop.

"I'm not here to hurt you. You'll learn that."

"Why are you here?"

"You will see, eventually. But you need to have some faith and you need to learn to trust."

Trust. Trust is everything, the essence of my existence. Does he know this? Some of the things this man says are so personal that I wonder if he's read a personal file on me. A thousand thoughts run through my mind at once and they all come back to one: has Sam been interrogated and buckled under the stress?

Turning to face him, I try to relax.

"What will they do to me today?"

"Try not to think about it."

"Trust works both ways. I have asked, and I know that you can answer me."

"Okay, they will test your trust in someone today. Have faith, Hun. Not everything is always what it seems."

"What's that supposed to mean? How does that answer my question?"

Without any answer, he pulls me in closer and holds me tightly.

The second room didn't feel as if it was such a long walk along the tunnel as yesterday, but it was difficult to tell. The white light wasn't here today, and I'd been allowed to keep my clothing. I wasn't feeling as vulnerable as I had yesterday. This didn't stop my heart rate soaring out of control as I waited outside the door for a fate impossible to comprehend. For all I knew It was a different area of this underground hell.

As the door released and I looked inside, I could see a simple wooden chair central within the room. My companion, if that's what I can call him, asks me to sit and then leaves, the door whooshing closed behind him. Grateful that he's not removed my clothes today, I pull my jumper down over my hands wanting as much of me covered as possible.

Above my head, a fan begins to whir and it's not long before the air warms and a hatch releases above my head making me jump. Startled, instinct makes me look up as something drops towards me: snakes, squirming mid-air are heading my way. Making a dash to the side of the room, my heart feels like it's about to explode.

I hadn't noticed the fire before but there was one in the corner of the room. How hadn't I seen it when I entered?

Startled by a noise behind me I spin around in time to see Sam enter. He's carrying something in his right hand that rests against his leg. Relief shoots through me and I rush over to him. I may as well have run into a brick wall. His coldness startling, as if he doesn't know me. He's unable to look at me: instead he brushes past me and walks towards the fire. Bending he busies himself with the flames leaving me feeling stunned. Whatever he was carrying is now half in the flames.

"Why didn't you meet me at the station?"

"I did. I picked you up as arranged."

I shoot him a look as he turns to face me. Sam was the driver? He's part of this? How could he betray me? I'll never forgive him: the years of trust between us, vanished in this moment. Was he sat watching yesterday, while I nearly drowned? A cold shiver ran through me at this thought and hatred begins to take over my mind and my heart.

From his back pocket he produces a glove: a heavy-duty gauntlet and places it on his right hand. Briefly, he looks towards me and I see the pain in his eyes and am now confused. Walking towards the fire, he picks up whatever he's placed there and returns to me.

"You need to sit in the chair, Princess," he says while brandishing a red-hot iron bar in his hand. Is he going to use that thing on me? The man I trust with my life, and my heart, is going to burn me with a red-hot iron bar. How have our lives come to this? How could he have switched sides and be working for Jade? I should have seen this coming.

I shake my head: no. Grabbing my arm with force he drags me towards the chair and demands that I sit. There are no restraints to keep me there, just fear. From a hidden speaker that broadcasts into the room, Jade's voice pierces our silence.

"Welcome, Katie-Ann and Sam. Now we will play my game. If you co-operate nobody gets hurt. If you don't one of you will."

Frantically, I look around the room trying to locate where the sound is coming from. Sam is motionless, his stare fixated on me which is making me uncomfortable. I'm looking anywhere but at him.

"Kate, you need to tell me where Rachel Smith is located. Its paramount that I find her."

"I don't know. She went into the witness protection programme, Jade as you know. She then vanished. We have no idea where she went."

"Not good enough. Sam, burn her!"

Without a word, Sam walks towards me and reaches out with the iron bar. Fear engulfs my whole system and my bladder empties. The bar passes my left arm and Sam bends towards the floor – beside me, a snake is making its way across the room. The iron bar scorches its skin, creating a stench that makes me gag. Sam looks at me for the briefest of moments and raises an eyebrow. He's not here to hurt me. Yet he can't be undercover because Jade knows he's here – she's directing the conversation at him too.

The questioning continues until all six snakes are dead and the smell of burning flesh too much for my senses. Having vomited and heard Jade's laughter, I knew she was in this underground hell with us. Wishing Sam had his gun, and that he could just end this now and knowing he hadn't, there is no choice but to continue our fight. With no idea whose side Sam is on, I decide I'm very much on my own now.

My trust in all other humans, vanished.

Jade asks one final time, the question I'm unable to answer. Fear evokes every cell in my body and I hold eye contact with Sam. With no more snakes for him to kill there's only me left for him to burn. He returns to the fire and re-heats the iron bar.

Returning, with the tip of it glowing red, he stands in front of me. Tears streak down my cheeks, but I refuse to turn away from him. As I brace myself for the pain and the heartache and watch as he lifts his own top and holds the red-hot metal against his own skin. He doesn't scream, but the noise that comes from within him curdles the air: a growl from deep within his throat that echoes through the room.

Metal crashes to the floor and Sam staggers forward clutching his stomach. Speechless, I rush to him and catch him in my arms. It's the briefest moment but one I needed to restore my faith. Straightening up, he restores his composure.

"I'd die for Kate, Jade. You may as well just shoot me. I'd never burn her skin with an iron."

Sam turns to me and raises an eyebrow, just slightly before walking towards the door. I needed him to turn around, but he doesn't. The door opens, he vanishes out of sight and my new companion enters again. Silently, he holds out his hand until I stand up. With urine-soaked jeans I take the uncomfortable walk back towards my cell.

28

COMRADES

Sam and Liam had served together in the army. He'd never spoken of him to Kate before and little did she know but he'd been working with them for a few months now. Thankful for him to rely on right now Sam knew he would take a bullet for him. He hadn't asked where he'd obtained the gun he so desperately needed but he hadn't questioned his need. Within six hours, he'd shown up at his flat with what looked like a new pair of trainers tucked under his arm.

For the past couple of days Liam had been Kate's protector. Sam didn't think for a second that Kate would see it that way. Now, as the pair scan this underground hell for her they realise they've left it too late. She's nowhere in the building, all signs of life have vanished. Frantically returning to the hatch and taking the thirteen steps upwards towards the light and the forest floor, they're suddenly aware someone else is here. Their vehicle has gone: it's either been stolen or moved.

Instinct forces them both to drop to the ground. As they army-crawl towards the cover of the trees they survey their surroundings. Nothing stirs, yet in both their imaginations

Shadow has them focused in the sights of her gun.

When they've made it into the cover of the trees, relief is apparent on their faces. Knowing they need to travel north east and following signs from nature they look for lichen. Lichen, or moss, grows in the shade: England, being in the northern hemisphere means that they can gain a compass bearing by using the location of moss as magnetic North. Realising they'd edged the wrong way from the clearing, they had to loop inside the edge of the trees before heading towards to town.

Criss-crossing The New Forest are hundreds of public rights of ways: pathways that are signposted to villages and destinations of interest. Its not long until they're on the right track and heading towards help. A passer-by with a mobile phone would be useful as their phones were both in the vehicle.

As they walked they discussed possible scenarios. Their time in war zones together meant their thought processes were similar. Sam hadn't witnessed what they'd done to Kate on day one, and as Liam described her ordeal his stomach churned. Knowing how claustrophobic Kate is, his words were making his heart ache.

Unaware of the full history between Ashbeck and Kate, Sam was sure that this information may just save her life. Breaking into a run he has renewed hope at saving the woman he loves.

Reaching the police station, gasping for breath, the two men jump ahead of the line without apology.

"There's no time for explanation, this is linked to the shooting. There's been another kidnapping and we know where she's been taken. We need privacy and a phone number now."

Sam writes down his name, identification number, the telephone number for the Home Office and also Paddington Green police station. He apologises that he's not got his identification on him but any one of these people will confirm that he works for them and that he would provide his fingerprint for identification to verify who he is but this the length of time this would take might mean a woman dies.

People were staring and starting to murmur behind them and the two men were led through a door and into a room. After a short conversation with the duty sergeant a telephone was placed in Sam's hand: he'd been connected to Cornwall Police. Explaining the situation, giving the case number from the fire when Ashbeck set light to Kate's property last year and giving details of her torture ordeal this week and they listened. While he remained on the phone, they searched their database, the coastguard incident database and got a hit. There was a report of a burning vessel out at sea this evening.

Sam's heart sunk, and his muscles grow heavy. The telephone drops onto the table. Liam picks it up and takes over the conversation.

When he disconnects, he shares a little hope.

"Air sea rescue are out there searching now."

29

FLAMING

Waking, I'm disorientated. There's an unfamiliar feeling beneath me: a motion I'm unable to place that's making my head spin. Trying to establish my location is proving impossible in the darkness. I close my eyes and try to think. Whatever I'm inside is rocking from side to side and is also rising and falling.

My senses are kicking in and there's something else I'm beginning to detect. Distant voices. I'm unable to hear the words but believe they're male. Wondering what more Jade could want form me, I lay here thinking this might be the end. Feeling totally exhausted, a calmness seems to have washed over me and my fight vanished. That's when I know that they've drugged me again.

Trying to move my arms and legs, they're heavy and un-cooperative but I know there's a need to move if I'm to survive. From deep within me I muster the strength to move and roll onto my side. With my head spinning and my stomach churning I force myself into a sitting position and I'm suddenly convinced I'm on a boat.

I could be anywhere!

Taking a moment to assess my situation helps me to confirm this. Not only does the movement fit but the distant voices are drowned out by the sound of a motor approaching: as it comes closer the boat rocks as the water is disturbed around it. Staying only briefly, the second boat speeds away. I believe I am now alone.

It takes all my strength to stand and start walking: taking careful, slow steps in the darkness. As I do a very familiar smell begins to creep into the room. Smoke is filling the space. Simultaneously, I begin hearing the crackling of wood.

Reassessing my situation didn't sit well with me and I was now in a panic. Frantically trying to find the door I have no choice but to head towards to source of the smoke. Knowing that opening the door might blast me in the face with flames, I didn't see what choice I had. I needed to do something. This might be my only chance of escape and my time-frame could very well be minimal.

Edging around the room, I feel with my hands and prey that I find the door. When my hand comes across the handle, I pause for a moment and hope its not locked. Pressing down, it gives easily, and I crack the door open. Smoke rushes into the gap and makes me choke. Covering my face with my arm, I head into it. Stubbing my toe on a step, I almost trip.

Making my way up the steps, surrounded by smoke, I can now see the flames. They're taking over the front of the boat. I need to jump. Standing, glued to the sight I silently remove my shoes and jeans: they would weigh me down in the water.

With the past few days weighing heavily on my mind, the thought of almost drowning in that room and fear screaming in every part of me I move towards the edge of the boat, slipping slightly as I do. Taking a deep breath does nothing to steady my nerves as I step off the edge and plunge into the freezing February water.

Unsure what would have been worse. To burn alive or to drown, I tread water in the dark and watch the boat drifting as it burned and hoped it would attract some attention.

I knew I wouldn't last long out here tonight.

30

BODYGUARD

Waking to the sound of a mechanical beeping I force my eyes open. Disorientated I try to move and as I force air into my lungs they burn, making me cough. Wood scrapes over lino flooring as a chair moves somewhere to my left and I feel someone beside me. It's too much for me to take in so I close my eyes again.

"Kate," his gentle voice whispers. "Kate, you're fine they sedated you. Kate, wake up!" His voice was becoming slightly louder.

Reluctantly I re-open my eyes and turn my head towards what has become a familiar voice. For some reason my left hand feels heavy and as I lift it I realise something is attached to it. My eyes dart towards my hand as the blonde man takes hold of it. His eyes remain focused on my face.

"Kate, look at me."

Compelled for some reason to obey him, my eyes gradually move towards his.

"Where am I?" I slur.

"In hospital, you're safe now."

"Where's Sam?"

"He sent me."

"That doesn't answer my question!"

"I know. I have no idea other than he's gone away."

"Away where?"

"Kate, I don't know."

"Who are you?"

"Your guardian angel, sweetheart. I am to move heaven and earth to protect you, apparently. Not that you would think that after everything you have just been through."

"That still doesn't answer my question!"

"No, it doesn't," he says and despite having closed my eyes I can sense his smile. "Then answer it or leave me alone."

"Sam and I served together. These days I work for the same people as you. I've been assigned to protect you."

"Some kind of bodyguard?"

"Yes."

"My assigned bodyguard allowed me to go through hell?" Feeling myself coming around from whatever medication I'd been given my mind was becoming less foggy. The urge to fight back was emerging and he was in my line of fire.

"I was there for damage control, Kate. I had to follow orders. Sam would never have hurt you as well you know but he placed himself in danger by disobeying Jade in that room. He has had no choice but to disappear. Making the most of that situation, our boss has sent him undercover. We too have a mission when you're ready."

"I only work with Sam."

"Not any more you don't, not now the dynamics have changed. I've been briefed about Kerry. To date the Home Secretary, you, Sam and the interviewing officers know about that situation. It's being dealt with very quietly."

"Covered up, you mean."

"Imagine if this got out! There will be gradual statements releasing knowledge on a need-to-know basis. Right now, preserving the Ashbeck case is a priority for the sake of the survivors and witnesses."

"Ashbeck is dead. Yes, there are some loose ends. But we are investigating Jade and Kerry now. It appears he left Jade in charge of his affairs but what we don't know is how deeply involved Kerry is." I look him in the eyes before continuing, "I don't trust you, just so we know where we stand."

"I know. I will earn it just you see."

"Are you an investigator as well as my bodyguard?"

"Yes. Once you have the all-clear from here we are heading to our briefing and then I might earn a little trust."

"How did you find me? I was abandoned on a burning boat in the middle of the ocean. I don't even know where I am right now."

"You were off the coast of Cornwall, near a really small town called…"

"Polperro?"

"Yes. Sam wasn't present for the entirety of your ordeal. Only the part that he was involved in. He asked me to talk him through what you experienced, and he had one of his gut feelings. We went with it. He was here to make sure you were safe before he vanished."

"Whenever I turn my back, someone I placed my trust in has betrayed me. Sam had switched sides in that room and suddenly he knows where I am abandoned and that I'm on a burning boat. How?"

"There's a larger picture, so I'm told."

"You expect me to believe that?"

"They've put some toiletries and a towel in the bathroom if you'd like to take a shower. Sam had a bag of your clothes in his car which I have. He said you were moving in."

"You can wait outside."

"Kate, I didn't look before and I won't look now. Leaving this room is not an option. You're not in a position to protect yourself if you need to but I am," he says as he slides his jacket to one side revealing his hand-gun. "I am here to protect you so go take that shower. We need to get going."

Conforming to his demands seems to be what I did these days. Sliding out from under the sheet and blanket I ease my feet towards the floor and gradually become vertical. Light-headed and weak I take a few unsteady steps before he catches up with me.

"What's your name?"

"Liam," he responds as he gently takes my waist and walks me towards the bathroom.

He hits the power so the shower bursts into life. Standing, I stare at him. The sound of the water is terrifying me yet I long to rid my body of the saltiness from the sea. The thought of placing my head under the shower-head after all I have endured spreads fear through my mind and sends adrenaline shooting through my body. My hands start to tremble. A sadness spreads over Liam's face as he realises that I might not be able to face this simple task.

"Okay, leave your gown thing on and I'll strip to my boxers. We have this, alright. You hold onto me and I promise you will be fine."

"Don't let the water get on my face."

"If it does, we will wipe it away," he says as he places his gun on the toilet seat and strips down to his underwear.

Taking me by the hand he gently encourages me towards the water where I hold onto his shoulders. Gently taking each of my hands he moves them onto his waist,

"Hold my waist so its easier for me to help you wash your hair. It'll give me more room to move my arms."

Doing as I'm told does nothing to relieve my fear – my hands are shaking against his waist and my legs begin to tremble as he steps me backwards a little further. Talking to me the whole time, he tries to settle my nervousness. As the water gradually moves its way up my body towards my head the fear increases. Water reaches my head and seeps through my hair, sending me into extreme panic. Within an instant I wrap my arms around Liam's body. He allows me to hold him and when I don't let go his arms encase me and hold me tight. For the first time in days I feel secure.

"Kate, I'm going to reach for the shampoo."

He takes my non-answer as compliance and is soon massaging my scalp.

"Okay, hold me tightly and we'll wash the bubbles away."

Holding onto Liam I allow him to rinse my hair as a sense of panic begins to take over my mind. Quick to recognise my state of mind, he reaches for a towel and hands it to me. Wiping my face and rubbing my hair I stop the water from dripping on my forehead and cheeks. Trying to erase the memory of that room from my mind seems like an impossible task: tears burn my eyes as I fight for composure.

The feeling of the wet hospital gown against my skin is horrible and after handing the towel to Liam I reach behind me and begin to untie the tabs. Allowing it to drop to the floor I am now standing before him completely naked but unable to return under the water without his help. I reach my arms out and he just looks into my eyes.

"Please help me."

Silence falls between us as the man that had held me through the night against my wishes now steps close enough for me to hang onto him at my request. He had watched my fight for life as water dripped onto my face and into my airways and I now needed his help to stand under the shower. My arms automatically wrapped around him as the water hit my body. Reaching for the shower gel, he gently removes one of my hands and fills my palm with liquid. As it drizzles onto my skin, I catch him watching and with what's left in my hand I begin to run it over his chest.

Scooping me into his arms he pulls me closer to him and holds me tightly. His hands don't caress my body, instead he gently walks me backwards towards the water again and holds me there for a few minutes. My whole body, now trembling with fear, is still in need of washing. Reaching for the shower gel again, Liam gives me some more and squirts some into his own hand.

"I'll wash your back," he says gently as he massages my skin.

Pressing my face into his neck I begin to kiss his soft skin with passion yet he does not respond. Determined to gain a reaction I press my body even closer and slide my left leg up towards his hip. There is no doubt what is on my mind. Sliding his hand towards my leg, he gently presses against my thigh and removes it from his body. He hits the power button and the water ceases.

Releasing his hold on me he grabs a towel and passes it over. I wrap myself within it and give him a cheeky smile. I have no idea what had just come over me.

With only a hand towel to dry his own body, Liam does the best he can with what he has. When he removes his wet boxers I don't turn away, but don't stare either.

Silence had fallen between us as we prepared to leave the hospital which didn't surprise me – I'd pushed things too far and now needed to apologise for my behaviour. Still feeling frail from my ordeal, Liam encourages me to lean against him as we follow the corridors towards the foyer and out to where he's parked. His arm supports me with his hand resting on my waist – this man seemed to be forming habits with me.

His choice of car surprised me at first but as he unlocked his Mini Clubman, I had to admit to myself it rather suited him. I climbed in as he held the door for me. While I reached for my seat-belt he fussed over putting my bag onto the back seat and got himself organised.

"Liam, I'm sorry for my behaviour back there. I have no idea what came over me."

"Forget it. You've been through a lot these past few days. Just know that I'm here for you, okay."

"No, what I did was out of order and it won't happen again. I really am sorry."

"We've not met under normal circumstances and we were naked in the shower. Well you were and I may as well have been. Kate, I showed you empathy in a kidnap situation, we need to consider the possibility that you might have Stockholm Syndrome."

I turn to face him, stunned.

"I was trying to push you away in that hell-hole. It was you who was insisting that you slept on my bed with me in your grip."

"Look me in the eyes and tell me you weren't grateful for the warmth and I'll drop this."

He had a point.

31

IN PURSUIT

Hate seeped through Sam's veins with every heart-beat at the thought of leaving Kate with Liam. He'd seen the way he'd looked at her in the hospital and knew him well enough to realise he'd be making a move on her if he got the chance.

Soldier to soldier they had respect but in truth Sam had never liked him as a person. Liam was always seeking to take what wasn't his and now he'd been assigned to protect Kate while he went deep undercover on a secret mission. Knowing full well that Kate would be angry he'd left when she was feeling so vulnerable incensed him. Despite their personal relationship having been affected, she'd supported him after Charlie's death. Now he couldn't be there for her. A marked man, he had to put Kate's safety before their relationship.

This undercover mission is his first without Phil Andrew's input. They'd either partnered or Phil had sent him under. Direct orders from the Home Secretary had meant that there wasn't really any choice despite the sadness it evoked and now he had to bury the negative emotions and get on with his job.

Waiting in Kings Cross railway station for the train that would take him back to Aberdeen, Sam sat with his rucksack between his feet. Within it was all that he would need. Now registered as a bodyguard for the Home Office he carried a concealed weapon under his jacket despite there being nobody to protect other than himself right now.

His mission was to seek and find Jade, to arrest her and bring her back to London. The world was closing in on this woman. Knowing she wouldn't come quietly, he knew it would be her death or his.

Challenges in this case had proven many and the ones facing him now were foremost on his mind. Jade would recognise him immediately. They'd worked closely together for years. She'd been responsible for changing his identity for the majority of his latter undercover cases. Handling all the data that he collected, she also knows how he operates. If she spots him before he knows he'd be the next coroner's case – there would be no hesitation in her killing him however crowded an area it was. From Jade's murder scenes he and Kate had been to, Sam knew not to underestimate Jade's gunmanship.

When his train finally showed on the departure screen, he picked up his bag and headed towards the platform. Boarding, he found his allocated seat and was thankful it was situated alone and with a table. It's always a bonus when sensitive data can be examined in private without the risk of members of the public looking over your shoulder. Angling his back towards the window, he holds the paperwork at an angle to ensure no one can view it as they walk past.

Grateful to have been busy for the entirety of the journey it had passed faster than Sam had anticipated. Aberdeen was the next stop, so he gathers his paperwork and neatens it so he can return it to his rucksack. Visiting Scotland without Kate was going to be emotionally difficult. Both of them shared personal memories here and he wanted her with him now. Yet he knew full well that this mission would test him. Having Kate here would hinder his ability to get the job done. He needed to be alone, to be vigilant and to kill in cold blood if it was required of him. He didn't want Kate to see that side of him. Not only hadn't she had the training, but she didn't have the stomach for it either.

Keen to check into his hotel with yet another identity, Sam joined the crowd with a baseball hat pulled down low over his eyes. Everyone rushed towards the barrier and out onto the street to disperse in various directions – he'd memorised the route he needed and made his way with purpose.

At the start of every new mission, Sam runs the streets at night. Never had he felt the need to do that with a gun. Yes, he'd carried before but this time it's different. Usually preferring to wear shorts he didn't want to attract attention in the cold February air so opted to cover his legs. It's a trait that Jade may be aware of so one he was keen to change.

Knowing that nobody knew he was here, other than the Home Secretary, gave him a confidence boost. The feeling he always got as his feet hit tarmac at the start of a mission sent a mix of emotions through his body: anticipation, excitement, expectation, anxiety, doubt and determination to name a few. Traffic was light. Each time he heard a motorbike engine in the distance his heart pounded in his chest with the anticipation that Jade might be approaching. Averting his face from view, he pressed on.

This mission was different in another way too. He'd never been asked to go under cover despite being the target. Never had he thought it would come to this. The risk was immense and unethical, but he knew there wasn't anyone else better for the job. When the Home Secretary had asked if he was willing to preserve Jade's life and Sam was unable to answer him, he'd just nodded. Deep down, Sam believed that was why he was here with a gun hidden beneath his hoodie.

32

THE PARTNERSHIP

Arriving from Cornwall, exhausted Liam and I walk up to my building and I key the code into the security system that opens the main door. It's not until we're in the lift that I realise I no longer have keys to my home because at some point during my kidnap I'd lost my handbag. Panic surged through me as this realisation took hold. Noticing the change in me, Liam started to fuss which I was finding annoying.

Strength in a team comes from being strong when the other needs you to be. Sam would take control of the situation and calm me rather than heighten it and Liam needed to learn how to do this fast if we were going to work together.

"I don't have my keys or my phone."

"We know and that's been taken care of. Sorry, I should have told you. Kerry had already made your place into a command post and that's continued while you've been away. You have new locks."

By the very nature of who I work for they didn't need my permission to take over my home when I wasn't in a position to give it. The thought that my belongings were at the mercy of strangers, however wasn't a pleasing one. My privacy is important to me and this crosses too many boundaries.

"Are the computers still in the kitchen?"

"Yes."

"And the wall? Is the wall undisturbed?"

"What wall?"

My heart sunk. I could feel the colour draining from my cheeks. What if Jade had accessed the wall before the command post had been taken over by the team?

"There's a locked room that Sam said was his son's room and that it wasn't to be disturbed. He ordered that nobody was to enter it."

"Did he give you his keys?"

Reaching into his pocket Liam produced Sam's keys and dangled them in front of me. This went a small way in relieving my anxiety. Taking them from him, I clasp them in my hand with mixed feelings – this very act had me doubting if Sam was coming home.

Approaching my front door, I reach towards the lock. Liam takes hold of my hand to stop me.

"If you never trust me again in your life please trust me now," he says as he knocks twice on my door.

The door opens and we're met with an armed response.

"Raise your hands above your head!"

Conformism seems to be what I had to do to get through the day. Both of us raise our hands.

"Oh, its you two. Come in."

Entering my flat, I'm astounded at how many people are here and don't recognise most of the faces. Jason Redruth is fast to appear and greets me with an awkward hug. Its his way of getting close enough to let me know that nobody else knows what's behind my locked door.

All I want is to take a shower and relax but that's too much to ask. Everyone is demanding my attention. They are wanting details of my experiences from the past few days to add to their data. Despite me knowing it's required I'm not ready to talk yet. I'm also not comfortable talking in front of so many people and know that I don't have to. My de-brief will be with who I say so. The Home Secretary and Jason Redruth can hear of my experiences. Liam can sit in if he wants, but he was there through the majority of it and I would suspect he will have a separate de-brief. His statement will confirm much of mine and will fill in the blanks from when my memory is blurry from being drugged.

Jason Redruth had given me instruction that he was to accompany me to Marsham Street. That meant the Home Secretary wanted to meet with me at Head Quarters. Liam would also need to be present but not for the entirety of the meeting.

He gave us both time to freshen up after our long journey. I chose a simple dark grey fitted suit with a white blouse and low black heeled ankle boots that I covered with a long black overcoat. It did nothing to hide how exhausted I look and I don't try to disguise that with makeup. Liam chose a black suit, white shirt with a tie. He looks very much like the bodyguard he says he is now. He was wearing a Kevlar vest too.

Interviewed, debriefed and the pair of us briefed on our new mission we are now heading back to mine. I need to pack what I need for a trip we are being sent on. With what is now expected of me, it's no wonder I need Liam by my side. I need to learn to trust this man – to depend upon him – quickly.

I've not been told where Sam is and if Liam knows he's not sharing that information with me. I hope they've not sent him after Jade because he will take too many risks looking for her. Imagining that he's running the streets of wherever he's been sent to learn the layout of the area, I have visions of a motorbike approaching with a woman brandishing a handgun at him. My body shivers at the thought.

Along with my new identity papers I'd been given a new mobile phone. Picking that up now, I head towards my locked door with Liam following me. There's something I need to do before we leave. I unlock the door and make sure that nobody else is in the vicinity before I open it. Letting him in first, I follow before locking us inside. I hold my finger to my lips to silence him. Taking images of the wall with my phone while Liam stands in awe of the work Sam and I have set out, I give him a little time to comprehend what he has become involved in.

Removing the key from the keyring before we exit the room, I ensure the door is locked before heading off to find Jason. I hold out my hand to shake his and place the key within it. Pulling him in for another hug, I too have a message for him.

"If I don't return, please use this. I trust you."

Liam had already packed what he needed, I'm not sure when he'd done that.

There was a car waiting for us outside and we both climbed into the back. The driver placed our bags into the boot. My handbag contained my passport and I assume Liam had his in a pocket. We were flying from London Heathrow Airport to Washington DC. Interpol wanted to meet with us.

In a specially concealed container I was carrying were DNA samples, tissue and bone taken from Ashbeck's body. Never before had I crossed borders with human remains. I hoped that the paperwork accompanying my morbid carry-on was in order and that it corresponded with my fake credentials. The consequences of it being incorrect were far to horrific to consider.

Our time with Interpol proved interesting. They were grateful for the samples but unsure if they would be of use with regards to connecting our crimes to theirs as DNA wasn't around in the seventies. However, the more information they held the more leverage they had. We all needed to form a positive link between Carl Ashbeck and Alec Johnson.

Interpol had traced the graves of Johnson's biological parents and having Ashbeck's bone samples for comparison may be enough to request an exhumation in court and would give closure to the families of his victims here in the States if a match could be found. The scientific jargon they'd blinded us with would have been better suited for JJ's ears and I'd be asking him questions upon our return.

We'd been given a guided tour of the facility and I have to admit it was impressive. Washington DC was just as impressive. It wasn't lost on me that Washington had been the location of

Johnson's first military revenge murder in America. The city is known for its connections with the Illuminati. Liam and I took a private tour of the city with an expert on the subject. Rupert provided great insight on the history of the city and of the perceived connections to the order.

I could see questions forming in Liam's mind and knew we needed privacy to talk this through. After our tour ended, we returned to our hotel rather than to Interpol. We'd used the excuse that our long flight had caught up with us and needed a couple of hours to re-charge.

Long discussions between the two of us at how this first military murder may have triggered the Illuminati connection saw that we had gained the same insight from our tour. The more we were learning the more connections we could make between the two identities. Later tonight I would share the images from my phone with Peter Stoneleigh, our Interpol contact. He wanted to meet us for dinner and I now believe he needed to view the rest of our findings, despite many of them being speculative.

33

POWER OF DISTRACTION

Sam emerges from his hotel onto the street and faces the bitter wind. His woolly hat is pulled low over his forehead and his shoulders are hunched against the cold. His right hand is deep inside his jacket pocket, his fingers wrapped around the grip of his Glock. It doesn't sit comfortably that his life has come to this – that he now wanders the streets with a gun in his hand and feels the need to sleep with one under his pillow.

There hasn't been any sign of Jade so far. Today he needs to hire a vehicle and head into the country to a location he knows she has purchased a house. He chooses a Land Rover for the simple fact it will fit in with the location of that property. He's never driven one before. This city case seems to be taking him into the country more often than he's comfortable with.

Approaching the property, Sam notices a motorbike in his rear-view mirror. The property itself is large. Set back from the road with a gravel driveway he has to wonder if it has a cellar. Slowing down slightly, he passes and watches the motorbike pull into the driveway. Finding somewhere to pull over he jumps out and jogs to the entrance, under the cover of the fir trees that line the perimeter of the grounds. A woman dismounts the bike, removes her helmet and turns her head. Moving back slightly so she does not see him, Sam hides from sight.

Jade has just looked directly towards him.

Sam sends a message to the Home Secretary giving details of his location and that he has sighted his target. He will sit tight and wait for her to ride out of the drive before he ambushes her.

Walking back to his vehicle, he starts the engine and turns it around before re-parking a little closer. Opening a window so he could listen for any movement he begins the long wait.

They want her alive. Sam wants her dead.

Six hours pass before any movement is noticed. A vehicle starts in the driveway. Sam places his gun on his lap and his mobile in his left hand. He starts his engine and pretends he's pulled over to use his phone, beginning a mock conversation to make it look more realistic.

A truck pulls out of the drive and turns the other way. A man is driving with a woman sat beside him. Sam takes a deep breath and places his mobile on his lap. As he does, he notices a sudden movement in his side mirror. Reacting without thought he grabs the gun and takes aim through the open window.

Jade is faster.

Slumping forwards against the steering wheel his body goes limp as blood starts trickling out of the wound in his face.

Jade jumps into the passenger side of the Land Rover. Unable to resist leaving her signature, she removes an ace of spades playing card from her pocket and tears it in half. Placing it on the inside of his shirt she gives a small smile. Reaching down and positioning Sam's foot on the accelerator, the engine revs loudly. She reaches her foot over to the clutch and puts the gear into second. As she releases her foot, she removes the handbrake and jumps out. As the vehicle begins to pick up momentum she stands watching. Crashing through electric fencing designed to maintain control of livestock the Land Rover starts making its way down hill. Sam is disappearing into the distance towards a stone wall.

The feeling of being jolted about shook Sam awake. It took every effort for him to lift his head, causing nausea and dizziness. Opening his eyes took even more effort. Taking him a few moments to realise he was still in the Land Rover and moving he tried to move his legs to brake. He couldn't. The pain in the side of his face was excruciating and it was all he could do to stay awake. A weakness was overcoming him. He felt damp – then he remembered the explosion. Jade's face clouded his mind. She had shot him.

All these thoughts were running through his mind as the stone wall got closer. All he needed to do was to brake but he couldn't work out how to move his feet. He'd forgotten how to drive.

Watching wasn't an option so he closed his eyes and hoped. Tears escaped from his eyes as Kate's image emerged in his mind. He wouldn't survive without her here to stem his bleeding. Charlie had died in Scotland and he was about to do the same.

The impact into the wall was hard. One of the wheels caught a stone and the vehicle turned onto its side, then its roof. Darkness fell once more in Scotland for Sam.

34

THE NEW MISSION

Liam produced our plane tickets on the morning we were supposed to be going home. We were flying back to London Heathrow but there was somewhere else we were heading. Although that was London, it wasn't home and there was potential it could take us anywhere in the world. I didn't like what he was telling me.

Jason Redruth had been chasing a man called Greg Kingston for years and he'd surfaced connected to our case. People he was associated with had disappeared and never shown up – they were assumed dead. Liam and I were going deep undercover in an attempt to discover what this character was up to. Jason now believed he was in direct contact with Rachel Smith and that he may have been the gunman who assassinated her husband, the former Deputy Commissioner.

We'd been assigned a new flat in London – with it came a new identity and a new start. Everything we needed was waiting for us there. He informed me that I was a member of a gun club and that he would teach me how to shoot a handgun – I wasn't impressed. I didn't think I could ever use a gun against another human and I know that was what he was asking of me.

Exhausted and in need of a shower Liam and I arrive at the flat that will be our home for the duration of this mission. I'm far from comfortable sharing a space with this man.

On the kitchen worktop is an envelope with a ladies' name on it. Stacy. Assuming that's my new name, I open it.

I regret to inform you that James Peterson has been admitted to hospital with a gunshot wound to the face, head injuries and significant damage to his spine. He is in intensive care. Please do not undermine your mission. We will keep you informed of any decisions made.

Frozen to the spot and staring at the message my body has gone numb. They have sent me undercover knowing that Sam's life is in the balance. I want to scream at someone down the phone and I want to scream at Liam. Opening my mouth, I try the latter. No words form so I close it again. Tears don't form, instead I stare at the piece of paper in my hand as if that will change the words.

So many questions rush through my mind that I want answering. I need to know if Sam will wake up and if he will know who he is, if he'll be able to walk or have permanent damage. This case has ruined the very essence of who we were as individuals and as a couple. Its destroying lives beyond ours and now its possibly taken Sam's.

"When do I start to learn how to shoot?"

"You've changed your tune."

"I need to look Jade in the eyes and pull the trigger."

"Woah. What's going on?"

I hand Liam the note and he tries to hug me. Pulling away from him I retreat to the furthest corner of the room and he gives me the space I need.

A tour of the flat reveals that we only have one bedroom. The last thing I want, or need, is to share a bed with Liam. I suggest we take it in turns – alternate nights in an armchair. He's having none of it. Placing a pillow in the centre of the bed he suggests that we stick to our side and we both have comfortable sleep. That our days are likely to be strenuous, stressful and lengthy and we should both get decent sleep each night. He is, of course, right.

My mind drifts back to the morning I left hospital and the advances I made towards him. Guilt pulls at my heart as I think about Sam and the state of his health and the fact he might not survive. I've no idea why I behaved the way I did other than the betrayal I felt Sam showed towards me during my kidnap. Had this case led me towards revenge this much?

Our first night in the flat had gone without a hitch. Liam shared the file on Greg Kingston. The speculation surrounding this man was circumstantial at best but there was more information than we had when we first started to investigate Ashbeck. Some of the locations were corresponding to those in that case and although I hadn't voiced my opinion yet, I would be doing so. We may be about to discover another depth to the original case.

Had bringing Jason Redruth into the investigation given us the lead we needed?

About the Author

Born in rural Essex, Donna grew up in a very competitive world surrounded by equine eventing. Seeking adrenaline-fired thrills throughout her life, she's also sailed at sea, ran marathons, canoed rapids and climbed mountains. Turning to writing after a serious head injury has enabled her to refocus her aspirations and set new challenges while finding the inner strength to overcome her injuries.

Broken, the first novel in The Warwick Cooper Thrillers series was nominated for an Author Academy Award and she travelled to Columbus, Ohio in October 2018 where she was delighted to be able to bring home an award in the Thriller category. The second novel, Betrayal in the same series has also been released.

Donna will continue to write crime novels, including one that is based on true events from her own life. Each convey her love of London, Scotland and often her home county of Essex. There is however a lot more than crime brewing in her mind. During 2019 readers can expect a very personal account of Donna's lengthy recovery, which includes poetry. She also has a huge writing project underway that will re-establish how she defines herself.

After reading Betrayal, Donna would appreciate it if you could take just a couple of minutes to leave a review on Amazon as this kind act truly helps an independent author with their career. She thanks you for your support and hopes you enjoyed her book.

For more information about Donna, please visit www.donnasiggers.com.

Also by Donna Siggers

BROKEN

Broken is the first in a series of thrillers featuring Katie-Ann Warwick and Sam Cooper. We join this dynamic duo as their relationship heats up and they have reason to work together again. Drawing on Sam's undercover experience to trace a kidnapped woman, Kate's friend and old colleague, they have every reason to suspect she's at the mercy of a prisoner who has just escaped – Carl Ashbeck.

Ashbeck has Kate on his agenda and very much in his sights.

Will Sam and Kate get the break they need or will the corruption within London's Metropolitan police hold them back? And, will Sam's past cast a shadow on the investigation?

Printed in Poland
by Amazon Fulfillment
Poland Sp. z o.o., Wrocław